Duone Ekane was born in Buea, in the south-west region of Cameroon. The book, *Kingdoms in the Heart of Africa* constitutes one of the fiction books she has written that focuses on Africa.

Duone Ekane

KINGDOMS IN THE HEART OF AFRICA

AUSTIN MACAULEY PUBLISHERS™

LONDON • CAMBRIDGE • NEW YORK • SHARJAH

A CIP catalogue record for this title is available from the British Library.

ISBN 9781398438101 (Paperback)
ISBN 9781398438118 (ePub e-book)

www.austinmacauley.com

First Published 2024
Austin Macauley Publishers Ltd®
1 Canada Square
Canary Wharf
London
E14 5AA

Prologue

Many kingdoms and empires have risen and fallen in Africa. Several years after the collapse of great empires like that of Mali, Songhai, Nubia and Ghana Empire, there was a sporadic emergence of four strong kingdoms; the Kingdom of Mbantuu, Kingdom of Manaka, Shanaba Kingdom and the Kingdom of Utanne, in a region, called the heart of Africa, that will rule and dominate the continent and the beyond. There were constant rivalries between these kingdoms as each sought to assert itself as the most powerful kingdom in the region. Due to this, suspicion prevailed amongst the kingdom, resulting in secret plots and alliances being formed between the different kingdoms. The existence of this tension between the kingdoms made the region beset with division and conflict. Despite this, in these kingdoms, a vast mass of minerals that had never been discovered before was found. The rise of these kingdoms will propel Africa to a place of prominence in the world. Unlike the previously fallen kingdoms, the new kingdoms knew the value of the resources they possessed.

Amongst the kingdoms, the Mbantuu Kingdom was considered to be one of the strongest and most feared of all the kingdoms. It was located close to a mountain with beautiful and scape scenery with a green savannah grass field and fertile soil due to the volcanic mountain that was located in the region. Mbantuu was a blissful kingdom, however, the kingdom was not always like this. The kingdom had in the past been plagued with a lot of violence and misery. There was constant conflict between the kingdom and its neighbouring kingdoms, particularly the Manaka Kingdom. The Mbantuu Kingdom was not only feared and respected, but it also set the pace for development around the region and beyond. It was pride for one to say they were from the Mbantuu Kingdom. However, the occurrence of an unforeseen circumstance would threaten its position in the region, leading to the emergence of a new order of power.

Chapter 1

Looking in despair around, was a group of young men lamenting about the state of their kingdom. One said, "I have to travel out of this place, there is no future for me here."

"Where do you want to go? We have to join forces to bring back peace and prosperity to our kingdom." One of the boys said to him. "So, you are just going to abandon the kingdom during these hard times instead of staying and helping to restore the pride of our beloved kingdom?"

Feeling anxious about what his friend said, he responded desperately, "What is there to save? Look around you," he said while spreading both of his hands in the air.

"All I see is misery and hopelessness. The smile that usually characterises the faces of our people is gone. All you see is dejected people."

The argument between the two was becoming heated as tempers began to flare.

"That makes you a coward, you are a chicken in that case. If you cannot stand strong in the face of adversity, then you are not a man," the boy said.

Not liking the direction where the argument was going, he opted to leave.

"Well, I cannot continue this argument with you, I have to leave now."

"Go away then, you are nothing but a coward, remember do not come back here again," the other boy yelled.

He then turned to the other boys and said, "We are going to overcome this situation. We are going to fight and rebuild the Mbantuu Kingdom."

He turned and looked behind him, as he watched the other boy leaving.

"We do not need cowards and chicken-hearted people, we will overcome this situation," he reiterated.

The boy leaving was Sango, he was the leader of the Mbantuu warrior group and the other boy chastising him was Mbanda. As he was leaving, hearing his friend's words felt like a knife piercing through his body, he felt rage building inside him, he knew what would happen if he turned back to confront him. He stood for a minute, trying to blank out the words from his mind.

*

It was a well-known fact that the people of the Mbantuu Kingdom had the lion spirit in them, which was often transferred to the first-born sons in the kingdom. Sango being the only son of his parents had the spirit in him. This spirit was attributed to be the reason why the Mbantuu warriors were ferocious fighters. Only the first-born sons of each family, who possessed this spirit were selected to join the privileged warrior group of the kingdom. The warriors were usually young, strong and muscular men who were tall and dark in complexion. They possessed extreme strength that surpassed that of the average Mbantuu man. Their role was to protect and defend the sovereignty of the kingdom from foreign attacks and uphold the supremacy of the Mbantuu Kingdom in the region of the heart of Africa. Once the young boys were selected to join the warrior group, their allegiance belonged to the king. They had a special hair style which they shaved, that looked like a rooster's comb. On the right part of their chests, were tattooed the head of a lion. Even though being the first son and having the lion spirit, this did not automatically mean that the young boys were admitted into the group. They had to undergo certain rituals and engage in wrestling battles as well as compete with the use of guns, swords, and bow and arrows challenges. Failure to pass these challenges dwindles their chances of joining the group.

Sango ended up being at the top rank of the group and became the main leader in command of the Mbantuu warriors. His assistant in command was young Mbanda, another good warrior who had an unorthodox fighting skills. The two did not see eye to eye and there was constant confrontation between them on various issues but mostly in relation to their differences in combat tactics on how to approach an attack. Mbanda was headstrong and believed in the usage of ruthless measures in fighting an opponent, whereas Sango had a more diplomatic and civil approach. Their differences often disrupted the execution of their tasks, which was often frowned upon by the king and his advisers. Mbanda often resorted to disciplinary approaches, and constantly challenged Sango's decisions. One day, while Sango was speaking to the warrior group, he was abruptly interrupted by Mbanda's intrusion, Sango fed-up with his antics said, "I think you should stop this behaviour of yours, it is not healthy for the group."

"And if I don't, what will you do?" Mbanda asked confrontationally.

Sango simply smiled and said, "Mbanda, I believe you know very well who I am. I'm simply, politely asking you to cease challenging my authority and orders in front of the young warriors. You know very well that if not for the respect I have for the king, I would have dismissed you from this group."

Mbanda stood quiet, while Sango continued, "All I am asking is that if you have anything to say or an input that is different from mine, or if you disagree with my ideas, you should simply inform me in private. It is as simple as that."

Mbanda, being one who did not like to be told what to do, still boiling with anger, began groaning and yelled in an angry voice, "I will not receive any orders from you anymore."

Sango trying to retain his composure said, "Well, that is up to you then, you can as well quit, there are many people in the group who will be willing and anxious to replace you. You know good and well that I have the ultimate decision on who I want to be my assistant. If you are posing to be an obstacle, you leave me with no choice but to pick someone else."

Realising that Sango was more powerful, Mbanda slowly calmed down. Seeing that Mbanda was calmer, Sango asked him authoritatively, "Do you still want to be my assistant?"

Mbanda replied timidly, "Yes I do."

"Good, then you should stop being problematic or else I will replace you," Sango said. He left him and went to talk to the other warriors.

After he left his kingdom, Sango struggled to travel beyond the borders of the region where his kingdom was located. After wandering for some years, he ended up travelling to the west. He had to work relentlessly to get to where he wanted, being a determined and assertive person, he knew he was going to get to the place he had set for himself. He was a charismatic person, and so people were drawn to him and were willing to help him. He had always been a person who was not afraid to venture into the unknown.

During his stay abroad, he had reservations about returning to his kingdom, he was apprehensive about how he would be treated most particularly by his friends. Life had been good to him. He travelled to the western world, acquired an education, had a good job and got married. He met a girl named Mbango, from a small neighbouring kingdom. They attended the same course. When they met, they were very ecstatic to finally find someone who came from the same region as them. They often met to share memories of their kingdoms and their dreams of returning to contribute to the development of their respective kingdoms. Apart from being from the same region, they came to realise that they had similar dreams and hobbies, this tremendously brought them closer together. They later had two sons, the first one was called Mbone while the second son, born four years later, was named Seme. The first son was a calm and collected child, when he was born, he did not cry. Sango and Mbango were concerned, thinking something was wrong with him. He did not speak until he was three years old, because of this his parents felt he was kind of special. The second son was the total opposite, he was very spontaneous, active and agile. Growing up, Mbone was very protective of his younger brother, they were close despite the differences in their personalities. After having lived abroad for many years, Sango became tired of life and longed to go back to his home land. He mentioned the idea to his wife one evening while they were talking.

*

Following the departure of Sango, Mbanda assumed the role of the head of the warrior group. He no longer had anyone to dispute his ideas and no one to challenge him. He had the chance to implement all the methods and ideas he had in his mind, and to do as he desires without any opposition from anyone. The group was structured in such a way that the other subordinate warriors did not dare challenge the orders of their leader.

With the kingdom plagued with famine and shortage of food supply and water, Mbanda resorted to engaging the warrior boys in illicit activities, notably robbery, which the king and his advisers were unaware of. The involvement of the group in these activities totally contradicts the purpose for which the group was created. They became involved in informal nocturnal activities, harassing people, robbing at night, seizing goods and taking the stolen items back to their kingdom. He did not have any concrete idea or strategy to suggest to the king on how to address the plight that beset the kingdom.

One day, it was in the afternoon, Mbanda had taken some of the warriors on their illicit activities as usual. They were hiding in the forest as they were anticipating to attack any group of people they saw passing by. While hiding in the bushes, in a distance they saw a carriage with some guards coming. Immediately, Mbanda recognised that it was a royal convoy. He was happy about this because he knew they were going to get lots of precious items. When the carriage approached where they were hiding, he commanded his warriors to stop the group. When they did, he emerged with a sword in his hands, looking fiercely at the guards who were all women and were in a fighting pose. He began striding towards the carriage. One of the female guards attempted to stop him, but he brutally pushed her aside. In the carriage, sat two women, a mother and her daughter who were wondering what was going on. The woman asked out loud to the guards why they had stopped. Her daughter peeped outside to see what was happening. The daughter turned to her mother and said, "Mama, I think we are under attack."

One of the female guards rushed to them and said, "My queen, we have been stopped by some warriors."

"Who are they?" they asked curiously.

"Don't they know who we are?" the woman who was the queen said in irritation.

She was about to get out to confront the men when her daughter stopped her.

"Ma, do not worry. I will handle the situation," the daughter said as she made her way out of the carriage before her mother could stop her.

When she got down, she adjusted her dress and started walking elegantly and seductively towards Mbanda. When he saw her, he began to grunt silently. He was perplexed by her beauty; he was looking straight at her face. As she was walking towards him, one of her guards attempted to prevent her, but she pushed aside her hand and looked at her, indicating that she should step aside. Mbanda stood motionlessly as he watched her approach him. He could barely speak as he was mesmerised by her beauty. The other Mbantuu warriors could not act as they were waiting for Mbanda's orders, they simply stood by and were watching. One of the warriors, who was standing closer to Mbanda whispered to him, "She is the princess of Shanaba Kingdom."

Mbanda nodded his head when he heard what he said. The girl came closer to him and began staring intensely at him in an enticing manner. She briefly looked around at all the other Mbantuu warriors that were there.

"Is there any reason why you stopped us?" she asked in a soft cajoling voice.

Mbanda, still intrigued by her beauty, could not utter a word.

She continued saying, "Should I then presume you do not have any reasons why? We are on our way to attend a very important event." She paused and went closer to him while still staring into his eyes and said seductively, "I reckon you don't know who we are."

Mbanda finally regained his senses and said, "You are the princess of Shanaba Kingdom."

She proceeded to say in a soothing voice, "Hmm, good that you know."

She moved much closer to him, as she was looking at his body and then his face. She said charmingly, "What a strong man you are."

She moved her right hand to touch his arms, while she was doing this, Mbanda began grunting and flexing his muscles as he was staring at her. Impressed by his reaction, she stretched herself to whisper in his right ear, "If you let us go my mother, the Queen will reward you handsomely."

"What kind of reward?" Mbanda asked.

"If you want to find out, come to Shanaba Kingdom," she whispered in his ear. She continued, "By the way, where are you from?"

Before Mbanda could answer she noticed the lion tattoo on his chest. She moved her right hand to touch the tattoo.

"I presume you are from the Mbantuu Kingdom," she said.

Short of words, Mbanda was merely watching her as she was caressing his chest. He seemed to enjoy the attention she was giving him. Realising that she had gained control over him, she swiftly removed her hands from his chest and quickly began walking away.

"You are invited to the Kingdom of Shanaba," she said.

Mbanda realising that she was leaving, swiftly grabbed her right hand tightly and pulled her closer to him while looking fiercely at her and said, "I will be there, trust me."

She giggled, indicating that she was pleased to hear that, and said, "That is great, see you then."

She looked at her hand suggesting that he could now let her go. When Mbanda did, she continued to walk in a seductive manner into the carriage. When she was in the carriage, her mother asked her, "Who are they and what do they want?" the mother asked.

"They are from the Mbantuu Kingdom. Do not worry, Ma, I have taken care of it," she said with a smirk.

Mbanda made a gesture to the other warriors to back down and make way for them to pass. The princess indicated to the guards to continue with the journey. As they were leaving, the princess waved her hand to Mbanda while he nodded his head in return. While all the exchange between the two was happening, the other Mbantuu warriors were wondering what Mbanda was up to, before this they had not spared anybody they attacked. When the queen and the princess had left, one of the warriors who was close to Mbanda asked disappointedly.

"Why did we allow them to leave without collecting anything from them?"

Mbanda turned, looked at him wolfishly, and then replied, "We will have other victims."

"So, we will go home empty-handed," he mumbled.

Mbanda, antagonised by what he said, grabbed him and said, "Are you now questioning my actions and authority?"

The warrior intimidated by his action replied, "No I'm not."

"Good, I thought as much," Mbanda said through clenched teeth.

He released his grip on him and yelled, "I am the supreme commander. You people will do as I say," he continued, "We are going to go back into the forest and wait for the other victims."

Chapter 2

Days later, Mbanda went along with some of his trustiest warriors to the Shanaba Kingdom to get the present the princess had promised him. The Shanaba Kingdom was renowned in the region for having the prettiest, strongest and most resilient women in the heart of Africa. It was also known for its colourful garments and jewellery that was admired by the other kingdoms. Besides this, the kingdom was unique because it was the only kingdom in the region ruled by a queen. Women were in control; they made the decisions and were the ones protecting the autonomy of the kingdom from external attacks. However, the Shanaba Kingdom had not always been led by women. The Kingdom during a fierce war against the Manaka Kingdom suffered a tremendous defeat that saw the death of the king and most men of the kingdom. It was a bloody and brutal war. The war led to the death of the king and all the potential men who were to succeed him. As a result, his wife assumed the role of the queen and ruler of the kingdom. The queen was renowned for her charm, beauty and for being witty. When she was crowned, she knew she had to build a strong kingdom with mainly the female population, since the men who survived the war were few and were rendered disabled due to the injuries they incurred from the war. She decided to build her kingdom on the strength of the women who constituted the majority of the kingdom's population. She embarked on training and building a strong female warrior group that was to be renowned in the region. She knew she had to devise means to preclude any future attacks from the different neighbouring kingdoms. The answer to this, she discerned, was charm. She decided to employ cajoling tactics which included enticing her opponents by the way she talks and moves. She used this to seduce the other kings who often lavished her with gifts and resources which she used in rebuilding her kingdom.

She was standing and watching her servants as they were taking care of the horses when she heard the voice of her daughter Enieg. She turned to face her.

"Today the warrior from the Mbantuu Kingdom will be coming here," the princess said.

"Ah, is that so?" the queen replied. "I remembered you told him you had a present to give him."

"No, no," the princess objected while moving closer to her mother.

"I said you, the Queen of Shanaba Kingdom was going to reward him handsomely."

The queen raised her eyebrows and asked, "What kind of present do you have in mind? Should we give him goats, pigs or cows? I heard the Mbantuu Kingdom is plagued with famine and hunger. Maybe that is why they are out in the bushes attacking innocent people."

"No, Ma, not that," the princess replied.

She went closer to her mother and whispered into her ear.

The queen yelled, "No, Enieg, not that!" while shaking her head in denial.

"I know you have crazy ideas, but that is totally absurd. Are you out of your mind? Marry him?"

Princess Enieg indicated to her mother to lower her voice.

"Shhh, Ma, it is not a bad idea," the princess said. "We need strong men in this kingdom. If I get married to him, we are going to have big strong children. It will be a great match. Mbantuu warriors are the strongest in the region, and we have strong women."

She paused while observing her mother.

"Think about it, Mother, I know you saw how strong, muscular and dark they are," the princess said.

She stopped as if an idea suddenly came to her.

"We are strong, charming and most of all beautiful women. They will be the most perfect children. They will rule this region."

The queen watching the enthusiasm of her daughter said, "It seems you have everything planned out then."

The princess took her mother's hand and said, "Yes, Ma, we do not have strong men anymore in this kingdom, all of them have died. We are only left with a few unfit men. We need strong men from the Mbantuu Kingdom."

"How are we going to achieve this?" the queen asked.

"Our charm, Ma, our charm, my queen," she said whispering as she left.

Her mother simply shook her head not believing what her daughter had in mind.

*

Mbanda and his men were waiting patiently as one of the guards had gone to inform the queen and princess about their presence. Both ladies came out to meet him, the princess was wearing a very colourful seductive dress. Upon seeing her, Mbanda stood motionless, staring at her. She had an enigmatic look. He was trying to say something, but his voice would not come out. He finally cleared his throat and said, "I am here to collect the present I was promised."

The queen looked at her daughter as the princess was making her way towards Mbanda. She stood in front of him. She stared at him deeply in the eyes. She then proceeded to place her hands on his shoulders and whispered something in his right ear. Mbanda began to grunt when he heard what she had said. She began smiling mischievously.

*

Days later, back in the Mbantuu Kingdom, the king was sitting with his advisers. He had been informed about Mbanda's illicit activities. The men were appalled when they heard it, this led the king to summon Mbanda. To find out if what he was hearing was true. He was informed by his advisers about this, and they had planned to meet at the palace.

"Good day, your highness," Mbanda said.

"Yeah good day, Mbanda," responded the king. "I assume you know why you are here."

Mbanda shook his head implying he did not know.

"Well, it has been brought to my attention that you are engaging in illicit activities," The king told him.

"I am sorry your highness, I don't know what you are talking about. What kind of activities are you talking about?"

Mbanda asked, pretending he was unaware of what he was talking about.

"You are involving the warriors in stealing and robbing people," the king said authoritatively. "Do you mean to tell me that all I have heard so far are lies?" the king asked him in irritation.

"I'm afraid I do not know what you are talking about," Mbanda reiterated.

The men in the room looked at each other in disbelief at Mbanda's response. Then one of the advisers said angrily, "Mbanda stop pretending! You know quite well what the king is saying." He continued, "Is it not true that you are taking the warriors of this kingdom to attack and seize the property of innocent people?"

Hearing this, Mbanda began laughing mockingly. "So that is what this is all about."

"Hey, watch your tone young man!" the king scolded him.

"Well, I am doing it because of the situation this kingdom is in right now. Times are tough, we don't have enough food, enough resources, and how do you people think we are going to survive? Our animals are dying, our crops are not doing well. That is the only option we have."

"Why can't you for once use your head? If Sango was here, this would have never occurred. You should stop the bastardisation of the warrior group!"

Hearing this, Mbanda became infuriated and angrily said, "Sango! Which Sango? Where is he? How can you compare me with that coward, who left in the face of adversity? He has brainwashed your minds with his lofty, quixotic ideas. I have been here; I have not left. By the way, I cannot stand here and continue this conversation, because it is futile."

He began walking out of the palace. The chief adviser of the king, seeing that he was walking out of the palace, began to yell at him to come back. He told him that leaving was disrespectful, but Mbanda paid no attention to what they were saying and continued to make his way out of the palace.

Chapter 3

One day while Sango was in a shop buying some presents for his sons, he accidentally bumped into a man who was also there. In the process of helping the man to pick up the things that had fallen on the floor, Sango looked at the man's face and asked curiously.

"Are you from the Manaka Kingdom?"

The man taken aback looked at him suspiciously and replied, "Have we met before?"

Sango answered, "No, I am afraid we haven't. I just assumed you are from the Manaka Kingdom because of the mark on your face."

It was the custom in the Manaka Kingdom that every member of the kingdom had to have a tribal mark on their face, which was performed when they were young. This was adopted as a customary trademark of the people, serving as a means to identify and separate them from the people of other kingdoms.

"Oh yes, I see," the man said while laughing. "And you are from where?" he asked.

Sango looked at him with caution as he did not know how the man would react if he told him he was from the Mbantuu Kingdom. After contemplating for some minutes, he said,

"Well, I am from the Mbantuu Kingdom. I know back home; our kingdoms do not get along and it would be impossible for us to talk like this."

The man understood what he was implying and replied, "Oh yes, I know," he brushed it off and said. "We have to leave those things behind us. We are all brothers. If you ask anybody in this shop, they will think we are from the same place. I am black you are black, I'm from Africa and so are you."

He began laughing while extending his right hand to shake Sango's hand.

"You are totally correct, it is good to see someone from the same region," Sango said.

They exchanged contact and promised to meet again later. When he got home, he informed his wife about the encounter. She was pleased to hear this, as they rarely met people from the same region as them.

Days later, Sango and the man from the Manaka Kingdom, named Njenne had planned to meet at a restaurant. Njenne came dressed in African attire, with gold rings on his fingers and a gold chain around his neck. He had a hat on his head. Sango was enchanted to see his attire.

"My brother things have changed. Oh! Things are no longer what they use to be," Njenne told him.

Sango sluggishly shook his head.

"My brother, you won't believe it that the Manaka Kingdom is now the leading kingdom in our region," Njenne informed him.

Sango, not comprehending what this meant, asked curiously, "How can this be possible?"

Njenne leaned towards the table and while bending looked around suspiciously to see if anybody was listening to their conversation. Satisfied that nobody was around, he then whispered, "Gold."

Sango, not sure he heard him well, asked, "You said what?"

The man repeated with the same gesture, "Gold, my brother."

He continued, "The Manaka Kingdom is now bigger and stronger than all the other kingdoms. How did we do this?" he rhetorically asked. "Gold, my brother," he said while raising his hands in the air to show Sango his gold rings and bracelet and laughing hysterically.

Sango was saddened when he heard this, he suddenly lost his appetite as thoughts began running through his mind. Njenne was talking continuously but he was not paying attention to what he was saying as his mind was somewhere else. As they were departing, Njenne informed him he would be returning to his kingdom soon. After they separated, Sango on his way home, felt a sense of guilt, he began blaming himself that if he had stayed in the kingdom and joined forces with the other young boys, his beloved kingdom would not be where it was at the moment. After being quiet, he suddenly said out loud, '*I have to return home, I have to go back and do something.*'

Later that evening, he planned on informing his wife about his decision. He was apprehensive about telling her because he was not too sure his wife would be willing to go back. However, he summoned the courage to break the news to her.

"Go back to where?" She exclaimed.

"Home," he told her.

She began shaking her head in denial.

"That was our plan, you remember how we had always talked about returning to—" Before he could finish his sentence, she yelled, "Yes, I know we had talked about this, but not like this, we have to plan and discuss the steps we are to take, you cannot just decide out of the blue because one man told you your kingdom has crumbled."

Sango attempted to move closer to her, but she looked at him indicating he should back off.

"What about the children? Did you consider them when you were making this decision?" she said.

"Trust me, I know what I am doing. I have made some mistakes in the past but this time around, I think I am making the right decision," Sango told her.

"How will the children cope and adjust? It is not that I am totally against the idea, it is just that the conditions down there as you said are deplorable," she said in a calmer tone while looking at him.

"I know but things are going to be better from what I heard today, if Manaka Kingdom can overcome the hard times, so can Mbantuu Kingdom," Sango said while embracing his wife in an attempt to comfort her.

"I did not mean we have to leave tomorrow or the day after, it may be in a month's time, two or maybe six months," he said.

"Or in a year's time," Mbango said. "Well, you have to tell the children because I will not do that," she said to him.

Hearing this, Sango began smiling.

He then said, "Do not worry about that I will break the news to them."

Later that day in the evening Sango informed his sons about his decision to return to Africa.

"To go back to where? Africa?" Seme burst out yelling.

His father sat quietly as he was observing their reaction to the news.

"What about my school? You want us to leave everything behind to go to some derelict kingdom. What about my friends, our life here?"

His elder brother Mbone sat quietly, he did not say much as they were watching Seme's outburst.

"Have you finished expressing your thoughts?" Sango asked his son.

Seme livid, was about to leave the room, to run to his mother who was in the other room when his father rebuked him.

"Where do you think you are going? You will sit down as we are having a conversation. I raised you better than this."

*

When Sango informed his wife about his desire to travel back home, they had decided to travel later. Several months later after he made the decision, he and his family boarded a plane that was taking them to Africa. He had managed to convince his sons who were not too receptive to the idea. Sitting in the plane, Sango's mind was already seeing himself in the Mbantuu Kingdom. He was filled with joy because he had for long envisaged about making the journey. He was ecstatic that he was going to see his beloved kingdom finally. It might not be the once beautiful and powerful kingdom he once knew, but that did not matter to him. After several hours of flying, they finally landed in the region and boarded a car that was to take them to the Mbantuu Kingdom. After driving through the rough terrain, they finally arrived at the kingdom. They were exhausted after the travel. Descending from the car that transported them, Sango stood in front of the entrance leading into the kingdom. Although he was tired, this did not stop him from feeling invigorated by the sight of his homeland. He closed his eyes and took a deep breath. His sons were looking around and immediately they saw the two big lion statues, they called their father. When he heard the screams of his sons, he opened his eyes.

"Look papa, look at the statues!" they said.

"Yeah, this is our beloved kingdom," Sango said.

They began to walk towards the statues for the children to touch them. The two lion statues were placed at both sides of the gate leading into the kingdom.

Sango said out loud, '*Finally, I'm home. Home sweet home.*'

His wife walked closer to him and held his arm. He looked at her and they both smiled.

"Yes, indeed home sweet home!" his wife said.

Sango carried their bags as he led the way, as they entered the kingdom. Sango was surprised that there weren't any guards at the entrance and that seemed strange to him. He knew guards were always placed at the entrance gate checking people entering the kingdom.

"Why is nobody guarding the gates?" he asked rhetorically. He continued, "It is easy for someone to enter the kingdom."

As they were walking further into the kingdom, he was surprised that he was not seeing anybody around.

"Is there nobody in this kingdom?" he asked. "Where are all the warriors?"

He stopped and began looking around. This was a total contrast to the Mbantuu Kingdom he knew. They kept on walking.

His wife then said, "Maybe they are at the king's palace."

"Maybe you are right," replied Sango.

After they had walked for about two hundred metres, they saw an old woman sitting in front of a house. When Sango saw her, he was a bit relieved. They walked towards her. Sango greeted her in the Mbantuu language and bowed down before her.

"Chan'mukan," Sango said, which simply meant "Greetings."

The woman responded and asked puzzled, "Who am I talking with? My eyes are not too good, so I cannot see you well."

Sango recognised whom the woman was then said, "It is Sango, the son of Baniag."

Everybody knew Sango and he was certain the woman would remember him.

"Sango," the woman said, trying to recall.

"Sango the command of the warriors?" she asked.

"Yes, Ma," Sango answered.

The woman began to rise from her seat to look at him closely and to be certain that he was telling the truth.

"Sango! It is not true. We thought you were dead!" she said.

"No, I'm not dead. I simply travelled," Sango told her.

"Yes, we heard that you travelled that is why Mbanda took over the role of the commander of the warriors, welcome back my son," the woman said.

The woman proceeded to hug Sango, as he introduced his wife and children to her.

"Where is everybody?" Sango asked.

"My son, the MbantuuKingdom is not what it used to be. Everybody has left. Most have gone to search for greener pastures in the other kingdoms," the woman said while shaking her head as they were looking around.

After they left the woman, they proceeded to walk towards the king's palace.

Sango was still astonished at what he was seeing as they were walking to the king's palace. When they got to the palace, it looked derelict, the compound looked bushy.

"It looks like the servants have also left," his wife remarked.

When they entered the palace, a young guard came towards them with a sword in his hands.

"How are you?" Sango said to him.

The guard with a stone face said, "Who do you want to see?"

Seeing that the guard was not in a good mood, Sango said to him, "I would like to see the king."

"Did he invite you?" the guard asked him.

"No, I was not invited," Sango replied politely.

"Well, the king does not attend to foreigners without any invitation. I'm afraid you people have to leave now."

"But I'm not a foreigner," Sango objected. "I am from this kingdom. I'm Sango," he said.

Seeing that his name did not ring a bell to the guard, he began to unbutton his shirt to show him his tattoo.

"See, I have the lion tattoo," Sango told him. "As you can see, I am a Mbantuu warrior too."

When the guard saw the tattoo, he knew at that moment that Sango was from Mbantuu. He began to apologise as he led them into the palace. He asked them to wait, as another guard who was there went to inform the king about their presence. The guard returned to Sango and informed him that the king would like to meet him. When Sango and his family made their entrance to where the king was sitting, the king rose from his seat and went to embrace him.

"Sango, my son. It is great to see you again; so many years have gone by. We thought you had gone forever," the king told him.

"It is a pleasure seeing you again," Sango told him.

One man who was in the company of the king said, "Sango, you are coming back when others are leaving the Mbantuu Kingdom."

"This is home. I had to come back no matter what," Sango said.

"I noticed that the place looked almost deserted," Sango remarked.

"Well Sango, things have changed, it has been long since you left, the Mbantuu Kingdom. The strongest kingdom in the region is unfortunately not what it used to be," lamented the king.

He continued, "There are still some people around, but they have gone to the fields to do some agricultural work. That is why it looks almost deserted."

"Let's not ruin your home coming with the sad stories, you should relax, we will have plenty of time to talk about that," the king said.

He turned and noticed Mbango and the boys, and said, "I guess this must be your family."

"Yes, this is my wife, Mbango and my sons Mbone and Seme," Sango told him.

The king greeted them and said to the boys, "I hope you boys are as strong as your father."

The boys smiled and nodded their heads in agreement to what he said.

"I hope you will enjoy your time here, Mbantuu is the best place to be," he said. "Well, maybe not now but later when things are better in the kingdom. I promise you."

"The kingdom looks dead and abandoned," Sango lamented.

"I could not agree more," replied the king. "A good number of people have travelled but there are still loyal Mbantuu residents who have vowed that whatever the situation may become, they won't leave the kingdom."

"I cannot blame them though because the conditions are dire. Who would opt to live in a place beset with water shortage, with crops not growing resulting in poor crop yield and hunger? Well, let's leave our discussion about the plight of the kingdom for another day, let's talk about something positive."

The king then ordered one of his servants to bring water for Sango and his family.

"So many years have gone by, you look different, you have a different hair style and new clothes, you have to change your clothes," the king said.

All of them began to laugh as the servant came back with some drinks for the family.

Chapter 4

Loud sounds of laughter could be heard coming from the palace of the Kingdom of Manaka. In one of the halls was the king. King Abuum was talking with his main advisers. He was a stocky man, who was very determined and ambitious. They were discussing the prospects of extending the territorial powers of the Manaka Kingdom. Being the main kingdom that was enjoying huge prosperity at the time in the heart of Africa, the king wanted to expand and broaden the kingdom's dominance and influence in the heart of Africa. The acquisition of smaller, less powerful kingdoms was the focus of the discussion the king was having with his advisers. The Kingdom of Manaka had for long not held a position of prominence in the region and it was an enormous pride to the residents of the kingdom that their kingdom was now determining the course of development in the heart of Africa. The taste of being in such a position of hierarchy felt sweet not only for the king but as well for the population. They, for once, walked with pride, something they had in the past envied about other kingdoms like the Mbantuu Kingdom.

"We should do everything to retain this position we have right now in this region," King Abuum said. He continued, "Manaka needs to be an Empire. I want this kingdom to be a great empire. I want it to be great like the empires of Mali, Songhai, Nubian, Kush and Ghana."

He paused and said rhetorically, "Why not greater than those great empires that had ruled this beautiful continent of Africa?"

His advisers were listening attentively.

"In order for us to achieve this, we have to conquer the other kingdoms and place them under our control," he said emphatically.

One of the men said, impressed by his ideas, "What a splendid idea, our king! You will be great like the famous Mansa Musa of the Mali empire."

The king agreed with him as they all began to smile about the idea that sounded tantalising.

While he was narrating his ambition to his advisers, he was striding back and forth in front of them, dragging his long flowing royal robe behind him on the floor. After he had completed his speech, he walked and sat down in a grandiose manner on his throne.

One of the men rose up and said, "And the Mbantuu Kingdom?"

The king answered dismissively to the idea, "Hmm, what about the Kingdom of Mbantuu?" he paused for some minutes. "The Mbantuu Kingdom would be more of a liability than an asset to my great scheme. The kingdom, I'm afraid, will not be beneficial to my empire. The land is poor, it is plagued with drought, and crops cannot be produced there."

He rose up from his seat and walked in front of the men, "I need strong kingdoms, kingdoms that will increase the strength of Manaka Empire, not weak kingdoms like

Mbantuu. As you know, a wild dog is better than a handicapped lion."

After saying this he began laughing, the other men joined him.

"What could be the cause of the plight of the Mbantuu Kingdom?" one of the men asked.

"Could it be that the kingdom is being punished by their ancestral spirit '*muakum*'?"

"That is the least of our worries and my worries, all I am interested in is making the Manaka Kingdom an empire," King Abuum answered.

"Our king, you are very smart and wise," the men yelled as they all began laughing and praising him.

*

Following his discussion with his advisers, King Abuum of Manaka Kingdom decided to pay the Queen of Shanaba a visit. The queen was in her palace unaware that King Abuum was coming to her kingdom. She was in her room going through her dresses to pick the one she was going to wear later in the evening. She was excited as she was preparing to see her daughter again. Princess Enieg and her husband Mbanda had travelled out of the kingdom and she was expecting their return that day. She was in a good mood.

"My beloved daughter will be returning home today," she said joyously.

"The princess has never been away for so long," one of the maids attending to her remarked.

"Yeah, six months since they left, she has not been away for that long. It will be great to have her back," the queen said.

"I know, she is going to have lots of tales to tell," the maid said.

"Oh yes, she will, she is not going to stop talking," the queen said, as they all burst out laughing.

"She has always dreamt of travelling to different parts of the continent—" she paused and continued "—I too had the desire to travel around but it has not been possible," the queen said sadly.

"But you can still travel, you are the Queen of Shanaba Kingdom," the maid told her.

"Yes, I know, well, it is not that easy, I have a kingdom to look after. I do not have the luxury to leave the kingdom for a long period," the queen said.

While the queen was in her room with her servants going through her clothes, a servant came to the room, panting.

The queen looked at her and asked. "Mehel, what is it?"

"My queen, the King of Manaka Kingdom is in the palace requesting to see you."

The queen, shocked by the king's presence in her kingdom, was silent for a moment, as she was staggered by the information, she then said, "What does he want? I do not remember sending or receiving any news of his visit. Tell him to wait, I am coming."

The servant left to inform the king what the queen had said. The queen continued to go through her clothes, unbothered about the presence of the King of Manaka. Twenty minutes had passed when she heard her servant knocking on the door again.

"Yes, what is it?" the queen asked in annoyance.

"My queen, it is the king, he said I should come and remind you about his presence."

"Tell him to wait," she said irritatedly. "I am the queen and I have to complete what I am doing before I can attend to him," Queen Edonge retorted.

"Yes, my queen, Should I tell him so."

The queen thought for a moment and said, "No, tell him, I will be coming down soon."

Minutes later after she had picked a colourful gown to wear, she made her way to the hall where the king was waiting.

In the entrance hall of the palace was the King of Manaka looking around the paintings that were on the walls. When he turned and saw the queen coming, he had a sly look on his face.

"The Queen of Shanaba Kingdom, the prettiest woman in the world," he said.

The queen gracefully made her way towards him to greet him.

He walked and grabbed her hand while looking at her in admiration.

"I don't remember sending an invitation to you," the queen said with a stoic face.

"No, No, I'm afraid you did not. I was simply passing by and I thought of stopping by to check on the most beautiful and intelligent woman in the heart of Africa," the king said. While walking closer to her and attempting to touch her face.

The queen brushed his hand away from her face and unfazed by his action said, "I presume you do not have any important thing to do than to come here uninvited."

King Abuum began to laugh in a sly manner.

"Nothing can be more important than coming here to see your beautiful face," the king replied provokingly.

The queen responded politely, "I'm afraid you may have to leave now because I have more important things to attend to."

"What can be more important than us discussing how we can join forces to make our kingdoms the greatest in the heart of Africa?" he asked.

Bemused by what he said, the queen with a total disgusted facial expression replied, "Oh please, stop hallucinating. I think you must be out of your mind—" she paused for a minute and said "—join forces with you? You must be insane!"

She continued saying between clenched teeth, "Your people killed my husband and other men in my kingdom and you have the audacity to come here shamelessly, with the ludicrous idea of joining forces with you?"

She clapped her hands and shook her head and said, "Are you a chump? You must be a chump."

King Abuum simply looking at her in an adoring manner, spread his hands out and replied, "Oh no, my dear queen, far from it, I'm perfectly in my right senses."

"The Kingdom of Manaka and the Shanaba Kingdom ruling the region of the heart of Africa—" he paused for a minute and continued "—does it not sound tantalising to you?"

As the queen did not respond, he continued, "Well, I said I should share this great idea with you." He went closer to her and said in a whispering voice, "Think about it, it will be great."

After saying this he began laughing hysterically.

The queen, unamused by this action, turned and walked away. In the process, she said, "You can see yourself out and please never come back here again uninvited."

King Abuum smiling cunningly said, "A beautiful woman like you should not be this cold—" he stopped with a smug look on his face "—a little charm won't harm."

The queen barely paid attention to what he was saying as she dashed out of his sight. King Abuum then indicated to his guards that they should leave while smiling mischievously.

*

A day after his arrival, Sango went to pay King Mualoko a visit. The king admired Sango a lot, he viewed him as a son. When Sango's parents died, King Mualoko assumed the role of a surrogate father to Sango. The king was amazed by Sango's ideas. He often consulted him on pertinent issues, because he considered Sango to possess wisdom far beyond his age. Although he had men who were his advisers, he was always interested in knowing what Sango thought. When he returned, the king was gleeful as he knew Sango was going to have some brilliant ideas on how to solve the plight that the kingdom had plunged into.

"What could really be the problem in our kingdom? The other kingdoms are prospering, but our kingdom is not. Is it the gods punishing us?" Sango asked.

"It could be a trial period, we must not lose hope," The king said. "Even though some of our people have migrated because of the drought, we still have some people in the kingdom."

"Yeah, that is good," Sango said, as it seemed he was thinking about something.

"Who is now leading the warriors?" Sango asked.

"The warrior group at the moment does not have a leader," replied the king.

Flabbergasted by what he heard, Sango exclaimed, "What about Mbanda!?"

"Ah, Mbanda, that prickly fellow. He was the one that championed the departure of the warrior boys. I heard he got married to the Queen of Shanaba Kingdom's daughter and he is now living there."

"Wow!" Sango said in disenchantment.

"So, they did not come back to the kingdom?" he asked.

"Come back?" exclaimed the king. "The boys after settling in the Shanaba Kingdom only came back to collect their families, since then, we have not seen much of them. They now call the Mbantuu Kingdom, *the doomed kingdom*," the king said chuckling.

Sango shaking his head in disbelief said, "Well, we have to find a solution. We are going to find a solution. My king, I can assure you, I will do all that is in my power to restore the pride and dignity of this kingdom."

The king simply shook his head.

"I will be going to the Manaka Kingdom tomorrow with some of the boys, they said they are going to buy some items needed in this kingdom, so I was thinking of joining them. I will think about what we have to do, as soon I as have an idea, I will let you know my king."

"I know you will," replied the king.

*

The next day at dawn Sango was preparing to travel to the Manaka Kingdom with some of the warrior boys. He was going along with his wife and sons. When he mentioned his desire to go to the kingdom to his wife, his wife informed him she was also interested in joining him on the trip. They took their sons along because they wanted them to see the area. They were travelling with horses and donkeys. The children were in a carriage that was led by the horses. On the way, they were amazed at the beauty of the landscape. They were thrilled that they were going somewhere. Their parents were pleased that the children, so far, have not been too miserable about coming to live at Mbantuu.

"I am happy that they seem to be enjoying the trip," Sango remarked to his wife.

"Yeah, you know children adapt more quickly to new environments than adults, do you know that they already have friends?" Mbango said.

"Yes, they told me about that, it is nice at least there are some children around with whom they can play with," Sango said. He continued, "That will help in making them love being here."

"Yeah absolutely," Mbango concurred.

"Papa, when are we going to reach the kingdom?" Seme asked.

"In a couple of hours," Sango responded.

"Is it really that far?" Mbone asked.

"Yes, it is a bit far from our kingdom," Sango told him.

After travelling for about six hours, they finally got to the Kingdom of Manaka. From afar, as they were approaching the kingdom, Sango noticed a huge wall, he was wondering what it was. The closer they got to the kingdom's entrance that was when he realised what it was. It was a massive wall, built like a fortress. They met many people who were also trying to enter the kingdom.

"Wow, this is huge," Sango remarked while staring at the wall.

The residents of the Manaka Kingdom under the orders of their king had built a wall around their kingdom. It was intended to protect the kingdom from any invasion. There were guards watching and checking anybody entering the kingdom. Before anyone is allowed into the kingdom, they had to have a pass provided to them by the guards, who were huge and muscular men.

When one of the warrior boys heard what Sango said, he turned to him and said, "Impressive? Wait till we get into the kingdom. These people have transformed their kingdom totally."

After obtaining their passes from the guards, they made their way into the kingdom's gate. As they were walking, Sango held the hands of his sons. The guards were not the only ones guarding the entrance into the kingdom, there were also leopards that were in cages. Since the place was jammed with people, they had to struggle to make their way through the crowd. The children were scared when they saw leopards, they held closer to their father. He told them not to be afraid.

"This place is a total contrast to the Mbantuu Kingdom," Seme remarked.

"There are a lot of people, Papa, where are all these people from?" Mbone asked.

"Most of the people are residents of this kingdom, some have come for commercial purposes like us, while others just came to visit," Sango told him.

As they were walking deeper into the kingdom they saw different beautiful sculptures, monuments and statues along the way. Mbango, being a lover of art, was quite intrigued by them. Arriving at the centre of the kingdom, there was a huge statue of a leopard. It was shining brightly under the sun. Mbone and Seme were thrilled when they saw it. They ran towards it to have a better view of it. Just like in all kingdoms in the region, the leopard was the sacred animal of the Kingdom of Manaka. The kingdom was well planned and had a beautiful unique architecture that was not found in the other kingdoms. As they were walking, further ahead they saw the statue of a man.

"Who is that?" the boys asked.

"It is the statue of King Abuum," one of the warrior boys answered.

Seme and Mbone began to walk towards it to have a look at it. They had never seen anything like it before.

"There are many nice things in this kingdom," Seme said.

"Yeah, that is true," Mbone said in agreement.

"Come on boys, let's be on our way," Mbango said as she pulled their hands along. "We will come back some other time so that you guys can look at all the statues and sculptures," she told them.

The warrior boys took them to where they normally did their transactions. After a couple of minutes of negotiating with the trader, they carried the goods they had bought. Trade was conducted not in monetary terms but based on the value of the goods and resources. As they were heading out of the market, the boys told them to hurry up because the market was about to close, and they had to leave before that, in order to avoid the crowd. In the process of walking, Sango accidentally bumped into a man, as he was about to apologise, he realised that the face of the man looked familiar.

"I think I know you," Sango said. "It is Njenne, right?"

The man struggling to remember him asked, "Yes and you are?"

"It is Sango, we met in the west," Sango told him.

"Oh yes, my brother," Njenne exclaimed. While laughing hysterically. "But you look different," he said looking at Sango.

"It must be the clothes and my hair," Sango replied.

"Yes, yes I see," Njenne said. He continued, "So you are back home."

"Yes, I have returned," Sango told him.

"Home sweet home," Njenne said.

"Yes indeed, no place is like home," Sango concurred.

"So, what brought you to my kingdom?" Njenne asked him.

Sango pointed to the goods that were being transported, indicating they came for commercial purposes.

"We are now returning to Mbantuu," Sango informed him.

"Oh, it is a pity, my brother. If I knew you were coming, I would have invited you to my house," Njenne said.

"Next time," Sango replied.

"Yes, my brother," Njenne said while laughing. "I'm sure you enjoyed what you saw in our kingdom."

They kept on walking while they were talking.

"Yes, I did. The Manaka Kingdom is quite impressive," Sango told him.

"Impressive is an understatement. It is hard work, my brother," he began laughing loudly. "Hard work pays, my brother," Njenne said. "I have to go to the palace to see the king, you know he is sending me on special missions," Njenne said proudly.

"Farewell then," Sango said to him.

"Do let me know when next you are around my kingdom, then I can invite you to my house."

Sango replied, "Yes I will, my brother."

"See you next time then," Njenne told him as they separated.

While Sango and Njenne were talking, Mbango and the children were looking at the things that were being sold in the market. As they were making their way towards the exit gate, the warrior boys saw a few of the boys from the Mbantuu Kingdom. They called them, and they exchanged greetings. Realising that the boys were from the Mbantuu Kingdom. Sango approached them. They greeted him respectfully, by bowing their heads knowing that Sango was older than them.

"Why don't you guys come back to Mbantuu?" Sango asked them.

"Commander, there is nothing there for us. At least in the Manaka Kingdom, we have a job and can support our families," one of the boys responded.

"Come back, let's rebuild our kingdom," Sango told them. "We need to come together and rebuild our beloved kingdom."

After they had talked, Sango and the others continued their way out of the gates of the Manaka Kingdom, they had to travel six hours back to the Mbantuu Kingdom. During the journey back, Sango's mind was still reflecting on what he saw at the Manaka Kingdom.

Chapter 5

A day after they returned from the Manaka Kingdom, Sango was standing in front of the house that was provided to him by the king, watching his sons as they were playing with some other children. Even though he was looking at them, his mind was calculating what he intended to do and what suggestion he was going to present to the king. Mbango came out of the house, she had been watching him through the window and she knew he was preoccupied. She walked out to talk to him.

"It's going to be okay," she said as she approached him and touched his shoulders.

Upon hearing her voice and feeling her touch, Sango turned towards her.

"Yeah, I know, it is just that I left this kingdom because I had a vision of making it a stronger and bigger kingdom in the region. Looking around at its current state I feel disenchanted by its current state. So many years have gone by since I left, I thought things might have ameliorated but rather things seem to have deteriorated and are much worse than when I left."

"Well, you had a vision, search deep inside of you. There is never a problem without a solution. Even though some of the ideas might not solve the problem entirely, they might help to augment the condition," Mbango told him.

"It is just that I have this idea, I do not know if it will work," Sango said staring at his wife.

"Eh, where is this self-doubt coming from? I have never known you to be a procrastinator. If you don't try the idea, you will never know if it can be of help," Mbango said staring at him questionably.

"Come on, put the idea into practice. You know everything, or every situation is not always bad. There is something positive in every situation. Maybe the situation besetting this kingdom is a trial period," Mbango said.

Sango looked at her trying to decipher what she was implying.

"Yes, maybe it is a phase the kingdom has to go through. Maybe it is meant as a test to see if the people of Mbantuu are resilient," Mbango said.

"Yeah, you are right," Sango said.

He informed her that he will be going to see the king later.

After his discussion with his wife, he decided to pay the king a visit.

"Sango, Welcome back," King Mualoko said.

"Thank you, my king," Sango responded.

"How was the trip to Manaka? I hope the children enjoyed it?" the king asked.

"It was good, the children loved it. They had a great time," Sango answered.

"I heard the kingdom has been transformed," King Mualoko said.

Sango looked at him surprisingly and said, "Yes indeed, it looks different from the Manaka Kingdom I knew. It is really magnificent, and the houses, monuments and statues are superb. You haven't been there my king?"

"No, I haven't been there. But I heard it is beautiful," the king replied. He continued, "I have not been able to travel that much to the other kingdoms."

"But why?" Sango asked puzzlingly.

"You see, Sango when you are the king of a once-prominent kingdom, people and other kings admire you and respect you but once the status of your kingdom declines, as the king, it is not easy to show your face in the presence of the other kings who once envied your position," King Mualoko answered.

"I perfectly understand, my king. That brings me to the next point I want to make. During my trip to Manaka, from what I saw, the kingdom is doing quite well," Sango said.

He paused before continuing, "I was thinking that maybe it could be helpful if you, the king, can seek assistance from the King of Manaka Kingdom."

The king was baffled by what he said and began shaking his head in disagreement with what he proposed.

"I, the King of Mbantuu? That is absurd!" he said in annoyance.

Sango, seeing that the king was not buying his idea, tried to convince him.

"I know it is difficult, owing to the relationship the two kingdoms had had in the past, but we at some point have to forget about what happened in the past."

He stopped as he was trying to put his words correctly in order to sound convincing.

"The condition in this kingdom is not going to be solved if we don't seek help from the other kings."

The king said slyly, "Or ask the gods and the ancestral spirit *muakum* for help."

Sango nodded his head indicating he partially agreed.

"My king, I'm sure you people have already done that. It's been many years now since I left this kingdom. I'm back and the situation in the kingdom is still the same and even worse. Think about it. There is no harm in trying," Sango said.

The king was still not quite convinced and was apprehensive that it would be propitious.

"I know it is a difficult thing to do, but would you not like to see the kingdom blossom again?" Sango asked him.

"Well, get to the point," King Mualoko told him.

"The best we can do is try," Sango said.

"Okay, we will do as you say, but I'm not too sure it will be of any good. I know that cunny King Abuum will be exhilarated by this," the king said.

.   *

While Sango was busy trying to find a solution to the problem of the Mbantuu Kingdom, in the Kingdom of Shanaba, Mbanda was enjoying his role as the son-in-law to the most powerful queen in Africa. He had always wanted to be in such a position. Following, his departure from the Mbantuu Kingdom, he had vowed never to return there. He had found a place where he was not only respected, married to a girl he had always dreamt of, but also, he was the commander of the warrior group and answerable to nobody. Even though he was a vicious and ruthless man, he was powerless when it came to Enieg, his wife. She was an enigma that intrigued him. He could not totally understand her, and this attracted him more to her. Knowing that the Kingdom of Mbantuu had fallen from grace to grass, under the influence of his wife Princess Enieg, they were planning to expand the influence of the Shanaba Kingdom. This, they thought required defeating or overthrowing the Manaka Kingdom's position in the region. The princess had always wanted not only to avenge the death of her father but as well the defeat the Shanaba Kingdom suffered from the Manaka Kingdom. Princess Enieg was the one championing this idea.

One evening while they were eating with the queen, the princess brought up the idea.

"Ma, don't you think it is time for us to avenge the death of the king and my father?" Enieg asked.

The queen hearing this almost choked.

"What! Where did that idea come from?" she exclaimed.

"Yes, Ma, as a payback to those people for what they did to this kingdom," Princess Enieg said.

"Are you totally out of your mind, Enieg?" she asked while looking at her sternly.

Mbanda was totally silent while they were talking.

"Do you not know that those people can massacre the entire Kingdom of Shanaba? We are barely recovering from the war we had with the kingdom. They are powerful not only in terms of resources but also in terms of the number of warriors they have," the queen told her.

The princess looked at Mbanda as if she was expecting him to chip in in the discussion, but he was mute.

"But we have warriors as well, we have the warriors from the Mbantuu Kingdom and we have our own warriors," Enieg said.

"Enough! Stop it. Don't make me lose my appetite," the queen yelled.

She turned to Mbanda and said firmly, "Talk some sense into your wife. I hope you are not the one inculcating these ideas in her."

"No, No my queen, I'm totally innocent. You know how Enieg is. She always comes up with some crazy ideas," Mbanda responded.

"Well, I was just thinking. What are our brains for, if not to think," the princess said.

"Let's complete our meal in peace," the queen told them.

Having been informed by the visit of King Abuum by his wife, Mbanda had been thinking about an idea he wanted to suggest to the queen.

"My queen, I heard King Abuum was here," Mbanda said.

"Yes, do you have a problem with that?" the queen responded.

"No," Mbanda responded.

She continued, "He said he wanted the two kingdoms to form a coalition, which I think is ridiculous."

Mbanda cleared his throat and said, "Well, I beg to differ, my queen."

The queen looked at him as if he was mad.

"We can use this opportunity, yes it can be a way for you to make the kingdom payback for what they did to this kingdom."

"How? I'm afraid I don't understand what you are trying to insinuate," the queen said to him.

Mbanda got up from his seat and began walking around the room.

"We can use them to reassert the Shanaba Kingdom as the leading Kingdom in this region, the heart of Africa. By joining forces with him, we can get to know about their ideas, steal them and later overthrow them. As they say, keep your friends close but your enemies closer." He smiled after saying this.

The queen was still not totally convinced about the idea, she said to him, "What makes you think he is not trying to do the same thing? He is not a fool, moreover, we do not have enough people to fight in case we intended to proceed with your crazy plan."

Mbanda smiled cunningly and said, "Leave that to me, my queen. I can make that happen. You are going to be in control of their resources and its people."

*

King Abuum was sitting in his palace discussing with his subjects when a servant came in and informed him that King Mualoko from the Mbantuu Kingdom wanted to see him. It was unusual for kings from the Mbantuu Kingdom to pay the King of Manaka Kingdom a visit since there has always been a tense relationship between both kingdoms. King Abuum was puzzled as to why King Mualoko wanted to see him.

"Did you say King Mualoko of the Mbantuu Kingdom is here?" he asked.

The servant replied, "Yes, my king."

"I wonder what brought him here, did he come alone?" he asked.

The servant informed him that he came with two men and a few guards.

"Hmm," the king mumbled.

He turned to his subjects and said in a rhetorical manner, "What could he want?" Without expecting any answers from the men, he said to the servant. "Okay let him in."

Outside of the palace, waiting for the return of the servant was King Mualoko, in the company of Sango and one of his trustiest advisers talking amongst themselves. They had come to see the King Abuum as Sango had earlier suggested. Their discussion was cut short by the servant who informed them that King Abuum has accepted to attend to them. Sitting on his throne in a conceited manner, was King Abuum, as he awaits the entrance of King Mualoko. When he saw his nemesis enter his palace, without budging from his seat, he raised his hand to indicate that they could have a seat after they had greeted him.

"So, what do I owe this visit?" he asked arrogantly. He continued, "It is unusual for the King of Mbantuu to be seen in my kingdom."

King Mualoko stood up as he began to elaborate on the purpose behind his visit. After he had completed, he went and sat down.

After hearing what he said, King Abuum rose up from his seat and began to walk around without saying a word for some minutes.

"Are you saying you came here out of the blue to request the King of Manaka a favour?" King Abuum asked sarcastically.

"Eh, as you are aware my kingdom has for long been going through some hard times," King Mualoko said.

"Oh yes we have heard," King Abuum said provocatively and began laughing as he was joined by his advisers.

"And my kingdom is flourishing," he added with a smirk.

Although he was not too pleased with King Abuum reaction, King Mualoko kept his composure and confidence.

"And what do you have to offer in return?" King Abuum asked. "You know I cannot afford to waste the wealth of this kingdom. Manaka is by far the most prosperous kingdom and I intend to keep it that way."

Being aware that he was going to ask this question, King Mualoko indicated to Sango to bring forth a bag he was holding.

"We have a present to exchange for the resources," King Mualoko nodded his head to Sango.

Sango opened the bag and brought out a magnificent sculpture, which was one of the most treasured items of the Kingdom of Mbantuu.

"This is one of the most treasured items of my kingdom as you know, this has been one of the things that previous Kings of Manaka Kingdom had been seeking to have," King Mualoko said.

Seeing the object, King Abuum and his men's attention was captivated by the object. He had returned to his seat; he got out of his seat and began to walk to where King Mualoko and Sango were standing to have a look at it.

"Hmm this is perfect, I have heard tales about it, but I had never thought I would see it," King Abuum said while staring at it intensely.

"Since we now have your attention, can we do business?" King Mualoko asked.

"So, the baobab tree has fallen indeed, eh?" King Abuum said condescendingly as he began to stride around while looking proudly at his palace.

"You see King Mualoko, this kingdom, my kingdom was built not only on the strength of my people but also by their mind," he said while pointing his index finger to his head.

"I had to change the mind of my people to make them feel they can be great, as great as the people of Timbuktu," he stopped and looked at them.

"Well, your kingdom used to be great. The resources discovered in this kingdom were just the incentive to motivate them, what is the use of having these resources when my people still think they are impotent? That they are not great? I had to inspire them to know that they need to work hard to build these beautiful buildings, houses, sculptures, you name it."

He went and was touching the walls of his palace.

"It is beautiful, isn't it?" he asked King Mualoko.

"I am sure you have done great things for your kingdom and its people," King Mualoko said as he was looking around the palace.

"Yes, and I'm sure you can do the same for your kingdom and its people," he said and paused for a few minutes.

"Unfortunately, I can't take that present."

There was total silence in the hall. King Mualoko and Sango looked at each other in dismay. He continued, "I would have loved to have it but it is something precious for you and your kingdom, I don't want to have something that has strong ancestral and spiritual powers attached to it. However, I will be willing to offer some resources as a gesture of good will," King Abuum told him.

The faces of the men in the palace fell, they looked totally disappointed with his decision.

"Fair enough, if you say so," King Mualoko said.

"I know in your mind you expected that I would be thrilled to have the present," King Abuum remarked with a smug grin.

"Well, I did not have any expectation on how you will behave, to be honest," King Mualoko said.

"Well, take it as a favour, but you may have to repay me sometime later," King Abuum said.

With that said he walked back to sit on this throne.

"In that case, we will be on our way now," King Mualoko said.

"My guards will see you out with the things you need, food or whatever," King Abuum informed him. He then indicated to his adviser to take charge of the situation.

As they were walking out, King Mualoko did not expect the encounter to turn out like this. He and Sango were shocked as they had expected the worst. It turned out better than they anticipated.

"That was a shock, I did not envisage him to be that nice," King Mualoko said.

"People can be unpredictable, the people you might expect to be mean may turn out to be the total opposite, and it is a good thing about humans at times," Sango remarked.

When they were out of sight, his advisers began to ask him in astonishment.

"My king, why did you not take the sculpture? It is a rare piece, you could have taken it and kept it, rather than giving them things without taking anything in return," one of the men said.

After hearing all their concerns, King Abuum brushed them off by saying.

"Ah my fellow people, calm down you can't always repay evil with evil, we might need their favour someday, even though the kingdom is wrecked now, maybe someday, it will be of use to our kingdom."

"But you had said you don't need them in your plan in making Manaka an empire," remarked one of the men.

Another added, "You also said that Mbantuu is weak."

"Yes, of course, I said those things but that doesn't imply the kingdom is of no use, it is always good to keep your enemies closer," he said while smiling.

"Relax my people, we have plenty, it doesn't hurt to give a token to the needy and starving," he said sarcastically.

Chapter 6

Following their return from the Manaka Kingdom, Sango continued with his quest to find solutions to the plight of his kingdom. He decided to trace the source of the river that used to flow through the kingdom, following a conversation he previously had with his sons who had suggested the idea to him. Early that morning, the thought dawned on him, and he informed his wife about his plans. His sons insisted that they wanted to accompany him. Together they left as the children were in raptures about the little adventure. That morning Sango had this deep feeling and conviction that finding the source of the river should be the focus of solving the perilous condition that beset the kingdom. Following their return from the Manaka Kingdom, the goods and foods that were apportioned to them by the King of Manaka for the residents of the Mbantuu Kingdom, were shared to the people by the heads of the different clans that made up the kingdom based on their clan membership. The heads of the clans were instructed to make an equitable distribution. Sango and his sons, after they left their house, headed to where the river used to flow. After a couple of hours of walking, they found themselves on the top of the hills. Sango was instructing his sons to be careful and to watch their steps. While on top of the hills, they stopped to have a view of the scenery of the kingdom, the view was breath taking, as they stood looking at the kingdom below. He had been on the top of the mountains a couple of times when he was younger, but due to an earth tremor incident that occurred that led to the death of some young men that went up to the mountain, most people in the kingdom became apprehensive to go there. Sango and his sons continued climbing, till they came to a spot he had never been before. The children were becoming tired and restless and he thought they should head back to the kingdom. As he was in the process of helping his sons descend the mountain, he noticed something that caught his attention. There were some blocks of stones in a distance, which triggered his curiosity. He began to walk towards the direction. It looked like a barricade. He was wondering what it could be.

Minutes later Seme said, "Wow papa this is unbelievable."

"Yeah this is cannot be possible," Sango replied.

Sango, caught up in his thoughts, said, "I can't believe my eyes."

*

Back in the kingdom, King Mualoko was standing in the company of three of his advisers as they were watching some young men digging a pit. Sango had some days earlier, given the king the idea that maybe the earth can be dug, in order to find out if there is underground water that can be used as a well. The boys were digging with all their strength, and tenacity. As the king and the men were standing watching the boys, came running towards them, was Sango and one of the king's guards. The men turned and looked at them as they were coming towards them, they were baffled with what the matter was.

"Sango what is going on, why are you running?" the king asked. Without waiting for them to respond, the king continued, "Has something bad happened to the children?"

Sango, still panting and struggling to catch his breath, said, "No my king, everything is fine."

After he had regained his breath, he began smiling and said with conviction, "In fact everything is great."

The men were looking at him with confused expressions on their faces as they were trying to comprehend what could be going on in his mind.

*

In the Utanne Kingdom, standing waiting with his back facing the palace and staring in amazement at the view below, was Mbanda. The Utanne Kingdom was located on the hilly and mountainous part of the heart of Africa. Unlike the other kingdoms, the people were very cautious of foreigners and did not take kindly to any act of invasion or intrusion. They rarely engaged in conflicts, even though they were very skillful fighters. They preferred to live simple and peaceful lives. The Head of the kingdom was King Duu, he had many wives and children, and he was a womaniser. He was in his early fifties and still looked very handsome and well built. His hair was grey and so was his beard that made him look almost angelic. Since the people lived on the mountain, they interacted very little with people from the other kingdoms. They rarely interfere in the affairs of the other kingdoms; however, the other kingdoms often sought assistance from them during times of conflict, which the King of the Utanne Kingdom often did not consent to.

"What breeze brought you here?" a husky voice asked.

He turned when he heard the voice, he knew who it was. He was in the process of walking towards the man when he was stopped.

"Hey, stop there!" the man yelled. "Our king wants to know why you seek to see him," the voice said.

Mbanda cleared his throat and said, "I have come in peace." He stretched out his arms outwards, to indicate he did not have any weapon on him.

Hearing this, the man walked towards him to meet him face to face. The man in question was the commander of the Utanne warriors, he was called Zuum. He had a hard face with tribal marks on it. Both men had in the past had a turbulent encounter that was characterised by a deathly fight between them. This was during the period when Mbanda was attacking and harassing people. He had tried relentlessly to expunge the encounter from his mind. He dreaded the feeling he felt within him when he looked at his face in the mirror and saw the scar that was inflicted on him due to the battle. He had for long held a grudge against the man that had left an ugly scar on his face, he wanted revenge because it deeply hurt his pride. He remembered the day vividly like it was yesterday. Despite having the great urge to retaliate, his passion died down the moment he married the princess of Shanaba Kingdom. The princess had succeeded in convincing him that revenge was not always necessary. She made him understand that the event was merely a price he had to pay for the atrocities he had done to other people in the past. Although Mbanda did not totally concur with this line of thought, he slowly accepted it, following some reflection. When the princess came up with the idea of attacking the Manaka Kingdom, he was at first not whole heartedly receptive to it, but later consented to it after some convincement by his wife. He knew which kingdom was going to assist them to accomplish their goal.

He embarked on the mission of going to the Kingdom of Utanne as part of the plan. He had hoped that whatever differences they might have had in the past; the King of Utanne would be willing to join in the plan. On the way, he was thinking about the commander that challenged him, it took a lot of courage for him to be going there to face him, not for the bitterness he had harboured within him against the man all these years, but for a more positive and productive purpose. They had not crossed paths since then, and Mbanda was not too sure if the man in question was going to recognise him but he was certain he did.

"I presume you remember me," Mbanda said.

"Of course, I do," Zuum responded.

"So, I see you are looking good," Mbanda remarked.

"Shouldn't I? The gods have been good to me," Zuum said.

"I have come in peace, contrary to what you might be thinking, I do not in any shape or form seek revenge. My visit is a peaceful one," Mbanda told him.

He motioned to one of his guards accompanying him to bring forth the present they had brought along.

He took it from the guard and presented it to the commander.

"If you permit me, I would like to present this to the King of Utanne," Mbanda said.

"What is the purpose of the gift?" Zuum asked.

Mbanda looked at him slyly and replied, "I said I'm here to establish a peaceful relationship between our kingdoms, didn't I?"

"Okay I will inform the king about your presence," Zuum said as he left.

While waiting, Mbanda was looking around the palace premise, watching the people who were working. Moments later, Zuum came back and informed him that the king would like to see him. Mbanda smiled when he heard the news.

While they were walking into the palace, Mbanda said, "I see your people have done a marvellous job in transforming this kingdom."

Zuum with a grimace replied, "I hope you are not thinking of coming back here to steal."

"Steal!" Mbanda exclaimed. "How low do you think of me?"

"Well, you were a thief before, what makes you not to be a thief now," Zuum responded.

"Oh, my dear friend, times have changed," Mbanda said twice while shaking his head.

Zuum looked at him unfazed and said while shaking his head, "Once a thief always a thief. I wonder why the great King of Utanne would pay an audience to a common thief from the Mbantuu Kingdom?"

Mbanda shook his head in disagreement, "Nah, no you got it all wrong my friend, point of correction, the prince of Shanaba Kingdom," he said with pride.

Mbanda continued with a smug face, "My friend, it seems you have been stuck on this mountain for too long. It is a pity you have no idea what is going on, down below."

He then said in a low tone, "In the low lands—" and then winked "—visit our kingdom you will not be disappointed."

Zuum burst out laughing. "Since when thieves like you are crown prince? Do they make thieves like you, the prince now? Have all the men in the Shanaba Kingdom died indeed like rumoured? I heard they suffered a great loss from the battle with the Manaka Kingdom, but it couldn't have been that bad. They must be really desperate, picking you of all people."

Mbanda brushing off his insults, responded confidently, "Yes indeed, I the great warrior of the Mbantuu Kingdom."

"Oh, spare me that," Zuum said as he walked towards Mbanda and looked at him straight in the face.

"Well, how do you like the scar on your face, Mr great warrior?" he said sarcastically while laughing in Mbanda's face.

Mbanda at this point was about to lose his temper, he was boiling inside with anger, but he was trying his best to stay calm. One could see on his face rage building up. The old Mbanda who was known to be a brute won't have tolerated such insolence from anybody, however, he was not led by his emotions anymore. He remembered what his mission was, and he knew he could not let the provocation derail him from accomplishing the purpose of his visit.

"Well, I must commend you for the scar, my dear friend. Hmm, it helped to change my life in ways you cannot imagine. As a matter of fact, it is why I was able to marry the princess of Shanaba Kingdom, she loves it. I am sure you know her, one of the most beautiful women in the heart of Africa." He paused as if he sensed that Zuum was shocked by his response. He looked him in the eyes in a confident manner and continued in a whispering tone, "She says it makes me unique."

"So, my friend," he stopped and touched the scar on his face. "You did a great service to me," he said as he burst out laughing and continued to walk into the palace. Zuum was dumb founded as he watched him walk away. Minutes later he followed him.

Making his entrance into the hall where the King of Utanne was sitting in the company of some men, Mbanda bowed as a sign of greetings. He waited for the king to acknowledge his presence before proceeding to walk towards him. One of the king's guards introduced him to the king.

"In your presence is Mbanda from the Kingdom of Mbantuu."

Mbanda corrected him by saying. "Point of correction from the Kingdom of Shanaba."

Where Zuum was standing, he simply rolled his eyes while shaking his head.

Sitting on his throne, the king asked, "Are you not from the Mbantuu Kingdom?"

"Great King of Utanne, I was born in the Mbantuu kingdom, but unfortunately I am no longer affiliated to it."

Zuum mumbled, "Hmm, I wonder why?"

Mbanda glanced at him and then continued to address the king.

"I am now the prince of Shanaba Kingdom, and it is on that account that I am here today," Mbanda said.

"If I may ask what happened that you left your kingdom?" the king asked curiously.

Not willing to divulge much about that, Mbanda simply replied with a smirking grin, "My king, conflicting interest."

"Such as…?" the king was about to ask when Mbanda interrupted him.

"The Queen of Shanaba sent me to you," Mbanda said, in an attempt to deflect the conversation from focusing on him.

"Hmm, the Queen of Shanaba Kingdom," the king said as he sat up straight in his chair savouring the idea. "Tell me, what does the beautiful queen desires from me?"

Seeing that he had the king's attention, Mbanda felt relieved.

"The Queen of Shanaba Kingdom desires to form a closer relationship between her kingdom and the Kingdom of Utanne," Mbanda told him.

"Hmm I see, that is a marvellous idea," King Duu said in an upbeat tone. He was becoming excited.

"If I may ask, why did the queen not come along?" the king asked.

"She would have loved to present the idea to you herself, but she had some urgent matters in the kingdom to attend to. She thought it was better that I, being her son in law, should be the best person to convey the message to you."

"Ha, ha, fair enough," laughed the king. "Oh, Queen Edonge of Shanaba Kingdom," he said in a dreamy manner. '*The most beautiful woman in the heart of Africa*,' he said to himself absent mindedly not paying attention to the others.

Mbanda and the other men were looking at him confusingly.

Zuum, realising what was going on, said, "My king, we are waiting for your reply to his suggestion."

"Oh yes, yes," King Duu said as he realised himself.

"It is of great delight to have such a union with the Kingdom of Shanaba."

He got up from his seat and walked towards Mbanda.

"It will be a great union indeed, what could any king wish for but to have close ties with a kingdom blessed with beautiful, powerful and wise women."

"Yes, I am sure it will, but I hope the king knows that the relationship will not be a romantic one," Mbanda said slyly.

"Of course not," the king responded dismissively. "Where did you get that idea from?" the king asked nonchalantly.

Mbanda was taken aback and could not respond but cleared his throat.

"Well, send my regards to the queen. It will be a great pleasure to see her beautiful face," King Duu said.

"Yes, I will, my king, I know she will be thrilled to hear that. I will be on my way now," Mbanda said as he began to make his way out of the palace.

*

In the Mbantuu Kingdom, Sango had led a group of young men up the mountain. Following his discussion with the king, he revealed what he saw up on the mountain. The king had ordered some young men to accompany him there. They were in raptures, they were smiling and walking triumphantly as if they had just returned from a victorious battle. Sango and the boys stood by with their tools in their hands as they were watching the water flow gently down the hills towards the kingdom. They had succeeded in pulling down the stones that had withheld the river for many years; the stones had diverted the course of the river, from flowing towards the kingdom. Sango felt great relief as he was watching the boys plunge into the flowing water. Their thrilling voices could be heard echoing from afar.

"Water! Finally, we have water in our kingdom," they were chanting.

"Our crops can grow now. Our kingdom has been revived," one of the boys chimed in.

Where he was standing, Sango was looking at them triumphantly. He had succeeded in unlocking one of the mysteries precluding the prosperity of his beloved kingdom. Words could not express how he was feeling. He was caught up in his thoughts as a result, he did not hear one of the boys approach him.

"Our great commander if not for you we wouldn't have seen the sight of this river again," the boy said.

Sango merely smiled.

"Look at the water flowing, all these years that we have been lamenting about the lack of water, meanwhile it was held back here on the mountains. Thank you, commander. May our Gods and ancestors bless and reward you for this great work you have done," the boy said.

Sango chuckled and told him, "I did not do anything, you guys did the hard work, and I simply saw to it."

"You are just being modest, if you did not see it, who else would have? Since you left nobody had discovered this," one of the boys chipped in.

"Well, it is a good thing for our kingdom, our beloved Mbantuu Kingdom, it is a gift for everybody," Sango told them.

They were in the process of descending back to the kingdom, when Sango, after looking around the area, saw something in a distance glittering. He began to walk towards the direction. Getting there, he bends down to have a closer look at the objects. He began digging the soil, he took the objects and held them in his hands.

"Could this be gold?" he said to himself as he was separating them from the ground.

I think this is gold, wow! Gold, he thought out loud.

There were other objects shining brightly. He looked at them closely, but he did not recognise them.

The boys heard him, one of them shouted, "Commander are you okay?"

"Yes, I'm perfectly okay. Come and see," he said.

The boys ran towards the direction he was standing and were looking on the ground.

"Wow! Is that gold?" one asked.

"You have discovered gold," they said in disbelief.

Sango was standing in amazement; he could not believe the incredible discoveries he had made in just one day. These discoveries will absolutely change the fate of the Mbantuu Kingdom for the better. This thought immensely pleased him.

Chapter 7

Queen Edonge was entertaining King Duu in her palace. The king had come to the Shanaba Kingdom following Mbanda's visit. He was looking forward to the encounter with the queen. He had ordered his guards to bring along special gifts, which he intended to bestow to the queen. Mbanda following his return from the Kingdom of Utanne had informed the Queen of King Duu's reaction to his suggestion. They all had a laugh when he narrated the king's reaction. Upon hearing the information, the queen decided to play along. So, the day that King Duu of Utanne came visiting, she made sure to look her best. When King Duu saw her, he began to panic and could not speak coherently.

Queen Edonge walked seductively towards him. She was dressed in an elegant colourful dress, with radiant pieces of jewellery on her ears and neck, which complimented her dark skin tone and a low haircut. She was looking fiercely at the king.

"King Duu of the Kingdom of Utanne, welcome to my kingdom," she said in a soothing voice.

The king began stuttering. "Thanks, Queen Edonge, the most beautiful woman in the heart of Africa."

"Oh, I'm flattered," the queen said, pretending to be blushed by his compliment.

"No, my queen, I'm not flattering you, it is the truth, there is no woman even in my kingdom as beautiful as you," King Duu said while staring at her in a mesmerising manner.

"I'm sure there are many beautiful women in your kingdom and in the other kingdoms," the queen said.

"No, my queen, you are just being modest. It isn't only about physical beauty it is also about the brains, that is what sets you apart from the others, you are not only physically beautiful but your mind and character as well," King Duu said.

"Hmm, if you say so," the queen said while raising her eyebrows.

Watching from close by was Mbanda and Princess Enieg. Hearing how the king was speaking, Mbanda and Princess Enieg almost burst out laughing but they withheld their laughter. Princess Enieg whispered to Mbanda, "Poor King Duu, it seems he has fallen for my mother," she said.

Mbanda looked at her and nodded his head.

"That is great for us," she said smiling.

Queen Edonge motioned King Duu to have a seat and requested her servants to offer him some drink. While they were drinking, the queen was telling him in more detail about the terms of the relationship. King Duu was totally smitten by the queen that he was barely paying attention to what she was saying. He was staring at her absent mindedly.

"So, do we have a deal then? King Duu," she asked in a calm tone.

Lost in his thoughts, King Duu did not hear her question.

"Hello, King Duu, did you hear what I said? Do we have a deal?" she asked.

Realising himself, King Duu answered without actually knowing what the question was.

"Yes, yes, of course, we do," he said while laughing shyly.

"Good that is great," Queen Edonge said softly as she indicated to her servants to fill their cups with more drinks, after which she walked to the king and made a toast with him while looking flirtatiously at him.

"Ah! And the deal is done, as easy as a one, two, three," the princess said to Mbanda.

"How did she do it so easily?" Mbanda asked.

"Charm, my dear husband, it is a Shanaba woman's thing," the princess said in a cocky manner as she touched his arm.

Foreigners had heard about the great wealth that was found in the kingdoms in the heart of Africa. In far distant lands plots were being made by these foreigners to travel to the region in a bid to grab these resources. The news of the resources had spread far beyond the borders of the African continent. The residents of the region were unfazed by foreign wealth or threats. The gold, diamonds and other precious stones and minerals found in the region were not solely perceived to be sources of wealth that belong to the kingdoms but rather as gifts bestowed to them by the gods and ancestors. Based on this reasoning they guarded and held the preservation of these resources as something imperative.

King Abuum of Manaka Kingdom was in the process of receiving some foreigners who had come to see him regarding the purchase of the minerals found in his kingdom. King

Abuum was a king that had grandiose ideas for his kingdom, he knew he could not accomplish his dreams mainly by limiting the market of his resources in the heart of Africa. During one of his visits out of the region, he saw the developments in other parts of the world, but he was determined that he had to make his kingdom unique and different by promoting a development approach that was akin to his region and context. This meant adopting new architectural designs and planning for his kingdom. He was not too keen on implementing foreign styles of construction. He believed in improving upon the traditional construction styles that were left behind by their forefathers. The kingdom had diverse minerals like diamonds and other precious stones. They were in abundance, and he had sent some of his advisers to go around to search for a market for their sale. The main buyers were foreigners who came to the heart of Africa, but he was becoming more and more strategic and apprehensive in dealing with foreigners.

Sitting on his throne, looking sternly as the foreigners made their entrance into the palace hall, was king Abuum. The men who were four in number were mesmerised by the work of art that was on the walls of the room. They could not believe their eyes at what they were seeing. They were walking slowly towards the king. They were stopped by the commander of the Manaka warriors because he thought they were getting too close to where the king was sitting. The men were looking a bit intimidated when they were in the presence of King Abuum. One of them, who looked much older and appeared to be their leader, inhaled deeply and began talking.

"Great King Abuum of the great Manake Kingdom, we have come to your kingdom on a special mission. We thank you for accepting to receive us, we have come in peace," the man said.

King Abuum merely nodded his head.

The man continued, "We have come here because we heard about the great wealth of the Manaka Kingdom."

The countenance of the king and the other men in the hall changed, the men realising this began to fidget and their leader stuttering said, "We are not here to take the resources."

He paused for a while as he was trying to figure out what to say next. "We have come from afar as you can see. We have come to find out if you will be willing to sell some of the precious resources to us," the man said.

There was a sudden uncomfortable silence in the hall, the men stood still as if they were in a trance. King Abuum was still quiet, his stoic face was beginning to make the men feel very uncomfortable and unnerved. The head of the king's guard then proceeded to say, "Have you finished talking?"

The man nodded his head and in a quivering voice replied, "Yes, I have."

Still not uttering any word, King Abuum indicated to his chief adviser to talk.

"So, if we understood you well, you people left your country, and came to our kingdom with the hope of acquiring our resources."

"No, not at all. We have not come to take any resources forcefully, but we have come to buy," the man replied.

"And if I may ask, why?" the chief adviser asked.

"We need the resources—" the man replied, he nervously continued "—we have money to pay for them."

One of the men came forward with a bag, indicating that money was in the bag he was carrying.

Looking least interested in what they were willing to offer, King Abuum leaned forward and said in his croaky voice, "We don't need your money, it has no use in the Manaka Kingdom nor does it have any use in the heart of Africa."

After saying this, he leaned back in his seat. The men looked downcast.

"What are we doing with your money?" the chief adviser said, chuckling. "It is of no use here."

The leader of the group, in an attempt to sway the decision in their favour, said, "We can offer other things, we have other things we can offer."

The commander asked, "Such as?"

"We can teach you, people, no let me rephrase it, we can teach your people some of our technological knowledge," the man responded.

"We do not need your technology as a matter of fact we do not need anything from you people. The people of the Manaka Kingdom are doing just fine. When you came into this kingdom did you not see our infrastructures? Did you not see the design of our houses and other infrastructure in the kingdom?" the chief adviser said.

"We are doing just fine. It was not built by foreigners or with the use of foreign technology."

The man said disappointedly, "It seems we have nothing to offer in that case."

"Good that you know," the chief adviser said. "As a matter of fact, you people may now leave the kingdom."

King Abuum did not utter any word. The men bowed their heads and proceeded to walk out of the palace. They were feeling that their journey had been futile.

Following the men's departure from his presence, King Abuum said to the men in his presence, "I don't trust them."

One of his advisers said, "Your highness but why don't we give them the chance?"

"No way!" King Abuum vehemently objected. "The more we open our doors to these foreigners the more likely traitorous strangers will come into our beloved kingdom wanting to steal from us. They are simply hiding behind the idea of buying the resources or teaching their technology to our people."

He stood up and began to walk while saying. "This kingdom was built on the genius ideas of Manaka people and not by any foreign ideas or technology. My people, our people are the only ones that will make Manaka a great kingdom."

Chapter 8

Sango was feeling very proud of himself as he was watching the piles of gold and the other new precious stones that had been discovered, being carried by the young men. In his presence, was his good friend Amueh, who coincidentally just returned to the Mbantuu Kingdom. He had travelled just like many other Mbantuu residents. Following the discovery of the new precious stones which were in abundance, the residents and the king named them *'Nnam'* meaning blessings, since they had no idea what they were actually called. Sango came up with the suggestion. Amueh was the same age as Sango, they were childhood friends. Unlike Sango, Amueh did not belong to the warrior group, because he was the third son of his father, and based on Mbantuu rules, only the first sons of each household were eligible to join the group. Amueh had always admired Sango, not only for his strength but also because of his wisdom. When Sango returned from his travels, Amueh was one of the people he had looked forward to meeting, so when he was told he was not around he felt dejected. Amueh was like a brother to him, since Sango siblings had died when he was young. He was the only child left, Amueh provided the brotherly relationship he needed. Thus, when he learnt that Amueh had returned to the kingdom he was over the moon. Amueh had brought along his wife and four children, three boys and a girl. It was a great time for both of them, they spent the time reminiscing about the glorious good old days of the Mbantuu kingdom. The return of Amueh was not planned as he informed Sango during one of their discussions. He had travelled to a distant small kingdom called Mongo, located in the western part of the region close to Cameroon and Nigeria. He had not heard about the discovery of the precious stones. It was a pleasant surprise to him.

"Massa, I just decided to come back to Mbantuu, it has been a long time, and I had to return even though things are not that good here. Since I left, I had no clue what was happening back here. Once, I met one of the young warriors when he was travelling by, and he told me about the devastation that Mbanda had done to the warrior group."

"You made the right decision," Sango told him.

"Yes indeed, I could not in my wildest dream thought that I will meet you here and that our kingdom will be blessed with these precious treasures," Amueh said.

The discovery of the new precious stones was considered to be a great treasure of the Mbantuu Kingdom. It marked a turning point in the fate of the kingdom. Sango saw this as a light at the end of the tunnel. It came at a time when all the options of reviving the kingdom were almost exhausted. The king was feeling quite relieved and exhilarated, he was beginning to regain the confidence he once had when the kingdom was vibrant. The king's advisory council had suggested that Sango along with Amueh, should be in charge of coming up with plausible ideas on how and what was to be done to the new resources. Sango, due to his travels, was considered to be more aware and knowledgeable on such issues and it came as a no-brainer that the men all consented about putting him in charge. One thing that was similar in all the kingdoms in the heart of Africa, was the spirit of togetherness and devotion to the prosperity of the kingdom.

In the Mbantuu Kingdom just like the other kingdoms, the residents viewed the prosperity of the kingdom as an imperative, which they were obligated to contribute to without questioning. When a child is born, right from a tender age, children are taught about being responsible for the success of the kingdom. Thus, growing up every Mbantuu resident pledged to die for the kingdom in the face of any attack. Greed and selfishness were gravely frowned upon, the feelings of oneness and being one's, brother's keeper was imbued at a tender age. The idea of stealing or keeping any resource for one's selfish interest was not tolerated. Anybody found guilty of engaging in such practice was severely punished and, in most cases, resulted in expulsion from the kingdom.

Looking at the shining objects in his hands, was Sango.

"They look pretty impressive," the king remarked.

Amueh was standing next to Sango as they were counting the bags that contained the minerals.

"I cannot believe how much quantity of these *Nnam* that were upon the mountains. It is like they were simply placed there by the gods," Amueh said.

"What are you hoping to do?" the king asked.

Sango as he was placing the stones in the bag said, "I was thinking that we can take them to Mbinze Kingdom. I have heard there are traders there who are interested in rare precious stones like these and sell them to foreign traders."

He continued, "Maybe I can go there with Amueh and some of the warrior boys with some samples of the stones to find out their value."

The king and the other men, after hearing what he said, nodded their heads in agreement.

"That sounds reasonable. Thus, it means that we have to keep these bags in a special room, where they will be safe," the king said.

The digging out of the precious stones, diamond and gold were shared by both the men and women. The men did the digging while the women separated the stones from the ground. At the end of the day, they all returned to the kingdom singing joyously.

Sango and Amueh were of the opinion that every son and daughter of the kingdom had to contribute to the reconstruction of the kingdom. They had suggested that news should be sent to inform Mbantuu natives of what had happened to the kingdom and that they should return; however, the king and his advisers vehemently objected to the idea.

Amueh chimed in, "Yes that is totally correct, and we cannot do this alone. I know a lot of our young men are working in the other kingdoms, they are contributing to the development of those kingdoms, and we need them here in our kingdom."

The king and the other older men were listening attentively to what they were saying but they were still firm on their decision.

"Why should anybody go to those kingdoms and inform them?" the chief adviser asked. "They left and never looked back."

"If they return on their free will, good and fine, but nobody is going to inform them or request them to come back," the king said.

"We had been begging them to come back, that the kingdom needs them, but all our requests fell on deaf ears. We were left with the old and feeble, on our own to fend for ourselves, while the young and strong men deserted us," King Mualoko added.

Sango, still trying to convince them, said, "We have a lot of resources up on those mountains. We have to exploit them before anybody out of this kingdom does."

Hearing this, the men became a bit concerned.

"No, nobody can take what is rightfully ours. If anybody attempts to steal from us, we must fight to death to protect what is rightfully ours," the chief adviser of the king said.

"I'm not saying that the other kingdoms are going to come here and exploit the precious stones without informing us. I was simply suggesting that we have to act fast," Sango said. "Anyway, the days of us fighting with the other kingdoms should be over by now," Sango pointed.

"So, are you suggesting we simply fold our arms and sit, if we are being attacked?" One of the king's advisers asked.

"No, no, far from it," Sango objected. "What I am implying is that right now we have to devise other means of asserting our place in the mighty region of the heart of Africa. This can be achieved through other means other than through wars."

"Such as, what other means?" the man asked anxiously.

Sango, feeling enthusiastic with the conversation, replied, "Hmm, persuasion and convincement, collaboration, forming a partnership and friendship with our old enemies."

"That is correct!" Amueh chipped in.

"Both of us have travelled far beyond the borders of our beloved kingdom as well beyond the heart of Africa. During the course of our travels, we have been able to observe and acquire experiences. In regions outside the heart of Africa, people are building their kingdoms and nations not by engaging in wars and conflict anymore," Amueh reiterated.

The old men were listening attentively to what they were saying.

"So, we are going to do like you guys have suggested, if it is in the best interest for the kingdom, why not," the king said.

While the others nodded their heads consenting to what he said.

"I do believe you have a better vision than us," the king said. "You people are young and knowledgeable about life beyond our region. So, it will be fair enough to trust your instincts with the precious stones."

After they had reached a consensus on what to do, Sango and Amueh left the king's palace knowing that the future of the kingdom rested on their shoulders. Sango, in particular, felt that he had a lot to do to turn the tides of the Mbantuu Kingdom.

*

In Shanaba Kingdom, Queen Edonge was addressing a group of women in a meeting held at one of the kingdom's halls located in the central part of the kingdom. The queen did not spend most of her time in the kingdom admiring her beautiful colourful dresses and jewellery, she rather devoted most of her time to uplifting the residents of her kingdom. Most often coming up with new development projects that she thought would be beneficial to the kingdom. She believed that the future success of the Shanaba Kingdom lied in educating and empowering the women of the kingdom. Like most kings in the heart of Africa, Queen Edonge as well had the vision of transforming her kingdom. She had as her primary goal to rebuild the kingdom following the defeat suffered at the hands of the Manaka Kingdom. She wanted the kingdom to be known not because of its beautiful colourful clothes, arts, jewellery and powerful women, but as well as a kingdom that promoted and supported creativity and the upliftment of both men and women.

Princess Enieg was playing with her children in the palace garden. The boys were growing big like their father. The queen who had been watching them through the palace windows, came out to join them.

"Be careful!" she said as she was walking towards them.

Enieg turned and looked at her mother.

"Mama, you are back," Princess Enieg said.

"Yes, I came back some minutes ago," the queen said as the children rushed to embrace her.

"How was the meeting?" Princess Enieg asked.

"It was great," the queen answered. "It is a pity you could not attend."

"Yeah, it is," Enieg said in a disappointed voice.

"How is she feeling now? I hope better," the queen asked.

"Yes, she is feeling better now as you can see, she is now able to play with her brothers," Princess Enieg responded.

"That is fine. The women in the meeting were asking about you. I know you are very passionate about things like that. The women had many brilliant ideas. We talked about expanding the agricultural activities as a means of diversifying the economy of the kingdom," the queen said.

"That sounds good," Princess Enieg said.

"Where is Mbanda?" the queen asked.

"He went with some of his boys to the border of the kingdom. I think he will be returning soon," the princess informed her as she was looking at her wristwatch.

"The children look big," the queen said. "They have grown so big."

"They get the big structure from their father. He constantly boasts that they have the Mbantuu genes," the princess said while smiling.

"I now see what you were talking about," the queen said.

"Yes, Ma, of course. It is like having the best of the region, strength, knowledge and beauty. Just look at their beautiful dark skin shining under the sun," Princess Enieg said with a sense of pride as she was looking at them.

"Beautiful my daughter, you have beautiful children," the queen said.

"Eh, that reminds me, what about the next step?" Enieg asked.

"With regards to what?" the queen asked curiously.

"About conquering the Manaka Kingdom of course," Enieg said.

"Oh, I have forgotten about that," the queen said. She continued, "I have many important things to focus on right now." While saying this she was walking to help one of the children who had fallen.

"I know mama, but you still have to rebuild the kingdom," Enieg said.

"There is still a lot of work left to be done. It is not wise to engage in such an act at the moment. Any attempt to do that will be disastrous and detrimental to our kingdom. We need friends right now not enemies," the queen told her.

Princess Enieg was silent for a while as she was listening to what her mother was saying, she was unusually silent. Her mother turned and looked at her and asked concerned.

"Are you okay?"

"Yes, I am, why?" Enieg said.

"Because you did not object to what I said, it is unlike you. I know you have been passionate about this," the queen said.

"Yes, Mama. Based on your arguments, I see your point," Enieg said. "Well, that does not negate the fact we have to avenge the death of my father and what they did to us."

"We just have to do it tactfully," the queen told her.

Princess Enieg paused for a few minutes, "Yes, you are right Mama," the princess said.

"I have this idea, we actually do not need to go to war with them, we just have to use our charm to get them to grant gifts to us which we can use in rebuilding this kingdom," Enieg said.

The queen was pleased with the idea.

"Yes, you see my daughter, our kingdom needs all the support and resources to be where we were before, and we don't have a lot of such resources right now," the queen said. "But we have done a lot with the resources we have."

Princess Enieg interjected, "The Kingdom of Manaka is blessed in abundance, so they can provide us with the resources without us paying much in return."

"Hmm, I don't think they will be willing to concede their resources without getting anything in return. We just have to give them the illusion that it will be an unconditional friendship between the two kingdoms," Princess Enieg said.

While they were talking one of the servants came by and took the children with her.

The queen and her daughter were sitting on some sculpture seats in the garden. There were beautiful colourful flowers planted in the garden.

"I'm thinking about organising a banquet in the kingdom. You know it has been a long time since we celebrated," the queen said.

The princess upon hearing this, jumped up from the seat she was sitting.

"That is great, Ma," she was beaming with joy.

"That will be so nice, we have to invite all the kings of the other kingdom. Oh, Ma, it is going to be amazing," Princess Enieg said.

"Enieg my daughter, calm down. It is not going to be a party for you," the queen told her.

But Princess Enieg was not paying any attention to her mother anymore as she stood up and began to stride across the garden in front of her mother.

"Mama, we have to look our best, all the top women in our kingdom have to look exquisite and radiant. That way the men from the other kingdoms will provide more gifts to us," she said.

"I'm organising the party to celebrate the great strides we have made after the ordeal we suffered from the war. It is our custom to thank the gods and ancestors for watching over us," the queen said.

"Yes, Ma, I know we will do it in honour of Father, my brother and all the great men, killed during the war," the princess said solemnly. "Mama, are you going to invite the King of Manaka Kingdom?"

"Well, it will be an attempt to extend an olive branch. We have to remember that the Kingdom of Manaka is the leading kingdom in the region," the queen said. "Moreover, if we want to have any form of repayment from them, this might be the best opportunity to gain the support of the king."

"Yes indeed, mama you are absolutely right. I cannot wait to inform Mbanda about this. Oh, what am I going to wear?!" she exclaimed.

Queen Edonge simply began to laugh knowing how excited her daughter could be.

Chapter 9

Mbango had adapted quite well to life in the Mbantuu Kingdom, even though she was at first apprehensive about living there, she had come to warm up to life in the Mbantuu Kingdom. since she did not know anybody when she arrived there, queen Anieh of the Mbantuu Kingdom took her under her wings. They spent a lot of time together as the queen taught her about the customs and traditions of the Mbantuu people. She was provided with traditional clothes that women in the kingdom wear. Mbango began to engage herself in the activities in the kingdom, she decided to introduce projects that would involve young people in the kingdom. Her goal was to introduce projects around the kingdom to promote creativity amongst the youth. She often travelled around the kingdom, organising classes in which she held talks to inspire them to build and construct things that were unique to the kingdom that could not be found elsewhere. She always said to them, "Use your minds, you are only limiting yourself when you limit your mind."

Together with Sango, they discussed the possibilities of expanding irrigation projects and digging wells in the different parts of the kingdom.

Sango was leading the group commissioned by the king and his board of advisers, as they were heading to the Kingdom of Mbinze. It was a small kingdom located at the borders of the region which was close to the sea. The Kingdom of Mbinze constituted one of the prominent trading centres where people from around the heart of Africa went, it was much smaller than the other kingdoms, but since it was located close to the sea, this gave it an added advantage for those, wanting to export goods and meet different foreign traders that could not make it into the interior of the region. Sango had thought it would be wise not to go to the Manaka Kingdom, in order to avoid any possibility of the news of the resources spreading and sparking any likely attack from the Manaka Kingdom and the other kingdoms. Joining him in the journey was Amueh and two young warriors. He considered going to the Kingdom of Mbinze as the better option since it was much smaller. Sango had placed samples of the precious stones *Nnam* in a bag tied across his shoulders. His sons wanted to come along but he refused since it was a business trip that had much at stake. The boys were disappointed, but he promised to bring something nice for them. On their way to Mbinze, Sango and Amueh were busily engaged in discussions about the different strategies that could be used to revamp their kingdom.

After several hours of travelling, Sango and company finally arrived at Mbinze Kingdom, late in the afternoon. Amueh knew one man who was a renowned trader. He was known for trading in precious stones, gold and other valuable resources. The boys who came along with them led them to where the man's shop was located. They had to struggle their way through the crowd to get to the place. The kingdom was located towards the western part of the continent, there were ships anchored on the shores. When they met the man they had travelled to see, he jovially received them. He was of average height and slim in build. He was sitting on a stool in front of his shop when Sango and the boys greeted him. He asked if they needed anything. Sango indicated that they should go inside his shop, since there were people outside and he did not want people to hear their conversation. The man led them into his shop. When they were inside the shop, they were looking around, there were different goods like clothes, art, sculptures and paintings.

"What brought you people to Mbinze Kingdom?" the man asked.

"We have come here to find out if you know what these minerals are?" Sango said.

The man moved closer to him as he was marvelled by them. With his mouth and eyes wide open.

"Wow! What are these? I've never seen these before. Trust me, I have seen a lot of amazing things, precious stones, gold, diamonds, you name it but these." He shook his head.

"I have never seen anything like them before, they look like rare stones."

Sango and the others were looking at him.

"So, do you know anybody who can buy them?" Sango asked.

The man replied, "Ah, buy stones like these: there are many people who would be interested in buying them—" he paused for a moment and said "—I think I know some people who would be interested to have them," he said with a smile.

"They will be willing to pay good money. If they are interested in them, my friends, your lives will be changed."

He began laughing and looking impressively at them.

"Yes, change," he said while laughing loudly with his eyes wide open.

"I could buy them if you people want to sell them."

He brought out his wallet to remove some coins, but Sango told him, "I don't think we want to sell them now; we have to do some research to have a good idea of their worth. I hope you understand; I'm not trying to be mean," as he proceeded to place the stones in his bag.

"Sure, sure fair enough," the man replied.

*

King Abuum of Manaka Kingdom had not forgotten his great ambition of expanding his kingdom into an empire. He had given his plan some thoughts on how to proceed with it after several months of discussion with his advisers, he had resolved that for this vision to be realised, he had to use tact. He had crossed out the idea of engaging in war with the other kingdoms but opted for a more civil diplomatic approach, that involved offering the kingdoms gifts. He had succeeded in accomplishing this with the smaller kingdoms around with their kings pledging their allegiance to him. War was not necessary, he thought, over the years, the heart of Africa had been beset with rampant conflicts and wars between the kingdoms that saw the death of thousands of people.

'Manaka does not need to fight anymore wars,' he said to himself. *'We need our people, they have to be strong, and many.'*

His advisers had the thought that he was going to wage war against the other kingdoms as a means to consolidate the Manaka Kingdom as an empire. He had objected to the idea. However, he did not reveal his plans to them. He left his advisers in suspense. One fine day, he decided to inform his advisers he was going to pay King Duu of the Utanne Kingdom a visit. His chief adviser, who was an old man named Molua, was baffled with the information. It was a common knowledge that the kingdoms in the region did not particularly had a very cordial relationship between them.

*

King Abuum left along with his guards to the Utanne Kingdom. His chief adviser was accompanying him on the journey. The old man was totally against the idea, but he could not do much but go along.

"Don't be too pessimistic, Molua," King Abuum said. "It is a courtesy visit nothing more. They are not going to eat us alive."

The old man was merely shaking his head in disagreement.

"Well, you know best. You are the king," he said.

King Abuum smiled at him.

After travelling for several hours, they finally arrived at the Utanne Kingdom. Seeing their convoy, this raised some concerns amongst the Utanne guards who were watching the entrance gate into the kingdom. It was not a normal occurrence that kings of the other kingdoms came to the Utanne Kingdom. Two of the guards walked towards them and stopped them. The leader of King Abuum's guards walked towards them. As they were talking, King Abuum was sitting in his carriage wondering what was being discussed.

"Don't they know that it is a king's convoy," King Abuum said, annoyed by the whole scene.

A few minutes later, the head guard of King Abuum returned as the guards of the Utanne Kingdom opened the gates for them to pass. As they were passing the gate, the guards bowed their heads. Meanwhile, the commander of the Utanne guards, Zuum, had been informed about their presence, he, in turn, informed King Duu. King Duu was in his garden watching his children as they were playing football. When he heard about the presence of King Abuum in his kingdom, he began to wonder why he had come to his kingdom. When he heard voices coming towards the garden, he sat down on a chair. His guards came walking towards him, when they got where he was sitting, he stood up in a bid to greet King Abuum who was walking behind his guards. The guards of both kings stood aside while the two men exchanged greetings.

"King Duu of Utanne Kingdom," King Abuum said as he opened his hands to greet him.

"King Abuum of the rising Kingdom of Manaka," King Duu said.

King Abuum while smiling interjected, "No, no my dear King Duu. It's the giant kingdom in the heart of Africa."

"Well, if you say so," King Duu said as both men burst out laughing.

After they had exchanged pleasantries, King Duu asked, "So, what brought you to my kingdom? It is unusual for the King of Manaka Kingdom to come to the Utanne Kingdom. I presume it must be something important."

King Abuum with a smug said, "Well, there is not much, I simply thought it is important that we should pay each other visits—" he paused and continued "—you know, it is not good that we don't visit our fellow kings. Afterall, we are all from the same region, the most powerful region in this big continent of Africa. I had an epiphany and I thought it will be wise that all the kings of the region should meet and break bread with each other."

"Fair enough. I think you are right. However, things are the way they are, because of your kingdom. It is your kingdom that has over the years created feelings of animosity amongst the kingdoms in this region. Your kingdom has been the troublemaker. It was your predecessor that attacked and killed the King of Shanaba Kingdom."

"You are perfectly right. I can't refute the fact that my kingdom is responsible for the tension that presently exists between the kingdoms. It is also good that you said my predecessor, I am not like the previous kings of Manaka. I am here to correct the wrongs they made. I am here today to offer an olive branch, to start a new phase in the relationship between the kingdoms in the region. To make new friends, and build new cordial relationship between our kingdoms," King Abuum said.

However, King Duu was not totally convinced by what he said. King Abuum sensing his scepticism, looked around and said, "Nice garden that you have here."

He got up from his seat, "Beautiful flowers. Are you not going to offer something to drink to me, at least let's make a toast to a new beginning in the heart of Africa?"

"Oh! Pardon my manners," King Duu said as he indicated to his guards to inform the servants to bring drinks for the king.

"Well, I hope your intentions are good and that you don't renege on your words," King Duu said to him.

"No, not at all. I am a man of my words. As you will come to see. I am a king with a vision for our great region. I cannot do it alone. I need friends and allies who share my vision. After all, my kingdom is the leading kingdom in the region," King Abuum said.

He got up from his seat and began to walk in a boastful manner and said, "I have all the wealth in the region. You know that your kingdom and the other kingdoms need me and not the other way around."

"I can see you are such a humble king," King Duu said with sarcasm.

Seeing that King Duu was looking pissed by what he said, he tried to change the tone of the conservation.

He said cunningly, "I did not mean to be condescending or obnoxious. If I came across like that. I apologise. I was simply stating facts. Like you know, our people often say the truth is not always pleasing to hear."

"You just can't help yourself, can you?" King Duu told him while raising his eyebrows.

"No, no, I did not mean it in a bad way," King Abuum replied with a grin and went to sit down.

The two men continued to talk for a while as drinks were brought. Several minutes later, King Abuum departed feeling satisfied with his visit, even though he had almost ruined it with some of the things he said, but both men ended up agreeing to build a friendship between their kingdoms.

Chapter 10

Following his return from the Mbinze Kingdom, two days later Sango and Amueh along with four Mbantuu warriors were returning back to the kingdom. This time around, they had taken a big bag containing precious stones, gold and diamonds. Sango knew they had to be cautious because the road to the kingdom was renowned to be dangerous as travellers were often attacked by gangs of robbers. To increase their security, two more boys were accompanying them. As they were travelling, they were suspicious of whoever they encountered during their journey. After several hours of travelling, Sango suggested that they take a rest in a small town called Batok, which was not too far away. The road that led to the town was a bit bushy. There were tall trees on both sides of the road. As they were making their way to the town, unexpectedly they heard sounds of rowdy voices as a gang of men emerged from the trees on both sides of the road. What he had been dreading had happened, Sango looked tense.

The leader of the gang walked slowly looking viciously at them, he had a talisman chain tied around his neck. Speaking in a loud thunderous voice, he said, "Bring out all your prized possession."

Sango looked at Amueh as thoughts were going through his mind. In the past he had had several encounters like this, he had been dreading this not to happen that day. He was devising strategies in his mind that would preclude the gangs from taking any piece of the precious stones, gold or the diamond. He muttered under his breath, "Not today! Not today."

The man heard him and said in a loud voice.

"What did you say?"

"I said we don't have any prized possession with us," Sango replied.

The man moving slowly towards him said calmly, "Are you sure about that?"

Sango without budging, looked straight in his face and replied, "Yes, I am."

"Hmm, then we will have to search and see for ourselves," the man said.

As the man was proceeding towards the direction that one of the boys who was holding the bag containing the precious stones was standing, Sango yelled angrily at him, "Stop there, I told you we have nothing important. The boy is only carrying some seeds in the bag."

The man looking pissed responded between clenched teeth, "I said we are going to see if what you are saying is true."

He continued as he indicated to his boys to move towards the boy's direction. Before he could make any attempt to grab the bag, Sango with all his strength rushed towards him, swiftly pulled him and pushed him to the ground. The other gang members, seeing that their leader was attacked, pulled out their machetes and cutlasses to retaliate. This forced the other Mbantuu boys and Amueh to bring out their weapons as well and a fight between both groups ensued. The gang leader because of the push began groaning as he got up looking furiously like an injured animal. He began to walk towards Sango in an attempt to knock him out, but little did he know what was awaiting him. Sango was standing with his hands clenched, was looking at the man as he was coming towards him. He on his part began to roar like a black mane lion whose tail had been stepped on. He felt all the special powers he possessed inside his body, suddenly woken up, and he immediately pounced on the man, hitting him viciously without stopping till the man fell on the ground with bruises and blood running down his face. The warrior boys on their part and Amueh were also defending themselves bravely from the gang members. They had succeeded in inflicting severe injuries on their bodies leaving them lying on the ground like their leader. Sango looked around him, realising that they had overpowered their opponents, walked to the man and looked at him lying on the ground.

"I did not want to do this, but you left me with no option. So, you people should from today refrain from attacking innocent people. Let this be the last time I see your face," Sango said.

He asked the boys belonging to the gang to pick up their leader and leave. While they were leaving, Sango said to them, "I don't want to see your faces again."

The gang disappeared into the bushes where they came from. Sango and the others felt relieved that they had succeeded in protecting the bag that contained the precious stones. They continued their journey hoping that they did not encounter any such groups on their way. Their journey to the

Mbinze Kingdom was void of any unwanted intrusion. Sango succeeded in selling the precious stones and collected the money paid from the sales, which they were commissioned by the king and his council of advisers to purchase things that were considered to be important for the kingdom.

*

Several months had gone by since the precious stones and other minerals were discovered in the Mbantuu Kingdom. Mbanda had not heard any news or any clue of what was happening in Mbantuu. His fellow warrior boys, who migrated with him to the Shanaba Kingdom had as well gotten married to Shanaba women and had children with them. They were living quite well, when compared to people living in the Mbantuu Kingdom. The thought of returning to Mbantuu had over the years rarely crossed his mind as he and the other men were quite complacent with the life, they were living in the Shanaba Kingdom. Whenever Princess Enieg asked him about going to the Mbantuu Kingdom. Mbanda would reply angrily, "I have told you several times that I'm not going back to that kingdom. There is nothing there for me."

"Why are you yelling, it is a simple question. Isn't it your kingdom?" she asked him. "Don't you have any good memories about the kingdom?"

Fed up with her constant inquiries, Mbanda said while looking straight in her face, "I have told you times without numbers, there is nothing there for me, my parents are here, my siblings are here, and I have nobody there."

"That is strange, so don't you want your children to see where you grew up? Don't you want them to know and see the kingdom that had been the leading kingdom in the heart of Africa or is there something you are hiding?" she asked him.

Mbanda was getting antagonised by her persistence, he simply yelled back at her, "So, all this while what I have been saying did not seem to get into your head?"

He paused for a while as she stood in a defiant pose.

"What are you trying to insinuate with that question? What are you hiding?" she asked.

He chuckled in a manner that showed that he was baffled by that particular question.

He began walking across the room, and said, "What am I hiding?"

He went closer to her and said, "When you met me, what was I doing?" Without waiting for her to respond he said confidently. "I was a warrior, a strong undefeatable Mbantuu warrior."

Hearing what he said, she burst out laughing.

"A warrior or a thief? The great Mbantuu warrior, tell me, which one were you?" she said sarcastically.

Mbanda began boiling up with anger. Princess Enieg was standing in front of him unfazed by his countenance. She was not the least intimidated by his muscles and height as she had over the years had discovered his weakness and how to make him feel weak to the point that he could not help himself. He simply did not comprehend the power she had over him. His rage slowly subsided as he looked at her, feeling powerless.

"Enieg, why do you always have to be mean," he said softly.

She simply stared at him without uttering a word.

Suddenly they heard a voice.

"Why are you people arguing?"

They turned and looked; it was Queen Edonge standing in the doorway. Unaware to them, she had been standing there for some minutes, she had come to pay them a visit. Enieg and Mbanda were living in one of the houses that were in the palace.

"It is nothing, your highness," Mbanda replied.

Not believing what he said, she said, "Nothing? I can hear your voices from afar."

"You know how Enieg is," Mbanda said to her.

"Well, whatever it is you should fix, and do not let the children hear you people shouting," she said firmly as she turned to leave the room. Minutes later, Mbanda left as well, as he was to meet up with some of his friends, while Enieg was left alone in the room.

*

In the Mbantuu Kingdom, Sango was busy planning and overseeing the construction projects that had been embarked upon by the residents of the kingdom. Following the sale of the precious stones, purchases were made for food supplies that were delivered to the kingdom, equipment for building a big well, and an irrigation scheme was initiated. A general reconstruction of houses in the kingdom, as well as the king's palace, was decided by the king and the leading men of the kingdom, to be preeminent. An entire new kingdom was to be constructed. Sango together with Mbango and Amueh came up with architectural ideas along with the best technicians in the kingdom. There was mass reconstruction taking place in the kingdom, and the people of the kingdom were working restlessly day and night without feeling tired. The air in the entire kingdom was characterised by delight and enthusiasm. Everybody, children, women, men, old and young, king, queen, practically everybody was involved in the reconstruction in one way or the other. Seme and Mbone were quite happy when the projects were started, this gave them something to look forward to everyday. They were extremely eager about the projects; they accompany their parents to the sites. They participated by helping in whatever small task that was assigned to them. King Mualoko, his wife and his council of advisers were as well deeply involved in the projects. During this period, the Mbantuu Kingdom was like a termite community, everyone was actively working to ensure that the transformation and revival of the kingdom was realised.

*

While the other kingdoms were deeply plotting against each other in an attempt to position themselves in a leadership position in the heart of Africa, the Mbantuu Kingdom was completely left out of this race, nobody was particularly interested in forming any alliance whatsoever with the kingdom. This however played out in its advantage. Since nobody wanted to be linked to the defamed and derelict kingdom, this actually was a blessing to the kingdom, as the kingdom was progressing under the radar, void of any preying eyes. Much progress had been made, the well was completed, the construction of the palace was almost finalised, and the irrigation scheme was completed. Sango was feeling quite contempt, he felt like a heavy burden had been lifted off his shoulders following the completion of the projects. Every resident of the kingdom was invited to a big feast organised to inaugurate the irrigation project.

*

News began to spread around the region about the newfound wealth of the Mbantuu Kingdom. The news about its new wealth could not be hidden forever, without the other kingdoms being aware of what was happening there. It was a fine sunny morning in the Shanaba Kingdom, it was the early morning hours of the day, and Mbanda was practising wrestling with some of his warrior boys, which was something he routinely did each morning. He saw it as a means to keep in shape. He was particularly keen on his physical appearance, although he was in his mid-thirties, he still had his muscles well-toned with a six-pack. After they completed their practice, the men sat down to rest a bit, while they were resting, one of the palace servants came by and informed him that a man from the Mbantuu Kingdom was requesting to see him. Mbanda was puzzled about who it was, he could not remember if there was anyone in Mbanuu that would travel a long distance to see him.

He asked the servant, "What did he say his name was?"

"He said I should inform you he is called Masango?"

Hearing the name, it did not ring any bell to Mbanda, he turned and asked the other men who were with him if they knew who it was. They were also not too sure if they knew him. At that point, Mbanda told the servant to bring the man.

Some minutes later, the servant returned followed by the man.

"Ah Mbanda, my good friend!" Masango yelled.

Mbanda squinted as he suddenly realized he knew who he was, "Oh Ekole! My brother, good to see you!" Mbanda said. "Did you change your name?"

"No, I have not. Have you forgotten, Masango is my second name, I prefer to use it nowadays," his friend said.

"But we know you as Ekole," Mbanda told him.

"Yes, I know," Masango replied.

"It's been a long time, my friend, you still look good after all these years, no big belly," Masango said while laughing.

"No, as you can see," Mbanda said. "You don't look too bad yourself."

"Well, what can one do," Masango said. "I heard you are now the prince of Shanaba Kingdom, you rascal! How did you manage to marry the beautiful princess of Shanaba Kingdom?"

Both men were laughing and smiling as they embraced each other.

"Well, it was my charm," Mbanda replied.

"Stop it, what charm? You, Mbanda that I know. I know the women of Shanaba Kingdom are very beautiful and charming—" Masango went closer to Mbanda and said in a low voice "—I do not mind if you can introduce me to one."

Mbanda began to laugh, and said, "Are you not married?"

"I am but it won't hurt to have a Shanaba woman as my second wife," he said.

"Do you mean to tell me, you came all the way just to find a second wife," Mbanda asked while laughing.

"No not all," Masango replied. "Are you not aware of what is happening in Mbantuu?"

Mbanda looked at him, with an expression indicating he was not too sure what he was implying.

"No, ever since I left, I have not set my feet there again," Mbanda told him.

"Hmm, no wonder!" Masango exclaimed. "My brother, you need to go there."

Mbanda shook his head in disagreement.

Masango continued, "So you have not heard?"

Mbanda looked at him in a perplexed manner and then said, "About what?"

"My dear friend," Masango said as he stood up. "Our kingdom has undergone an impressive transformation."

What he said caught the attention of Mbanda and the other two Mbanda warriors.

Mbanda while getting up asked, "How? When?" while looking at his friend and his two Mbantuu warriors.

"If you go there, you won't believe your eyes. It has been transformed completely."

"Transformed?" Mbanda said slowly.

"So, you did not hear anything about the discoveries?" he asked.

"Discoveries, what discoveries?" Mbanda asked.

He began to laugh. "My dear brother so you don't know about the precious stones, the *Nnam* of Mbantuu Kingdom," he said.

Mbanda and the other men were looking at him in bewilderment.

"Gold, diamond, and new precious stones that have never been seen before were discovered in our kingdom," Masango informed them.

There was a sudden silence as Mbanda, and his friends could not believe what they had just heard.

"Sango is back," Masango continued.

"Sango? Back in Mbantuu?" Mbanda said astonishingly.

"Yes indeed, he is the one who made the discoveries," Masango informed him as he took his glass to drink the juice that was given to him.

Mbanda and his Mbantuu friends face looked totally in disbelief upon hearing the news. In his mind, Mbanda was thinking about how he was going to go back to the Mbantuu Kingdom.

*

When King Abuum heard about the changes taking place in the Mbantuu Kingdom, he was a bit disappointed and jealous. He was seeing the new developments taking place at Mbantuu as a likely threat to his grand scheme of expanding his kingdom into an empire.

"So, what are we going to do?" his chief adviser asked him.

King Abuum was silent for some minutes as he was thinking about what to say, then he said, "Nothing, nothing for now," he responded while looking at his adviser's face.

The man looked disenchanted.

"Any attempt at engaging in any threat with the kingdom will be detrimental at this point to my plans," King Abuum said.

He rose from his seat and began to walk towards the window. He stopped and began to stare through the window.

"King Mualoko owes me, for the favour I rendered to him and his kingdom during their period of distress," he said while staring through the window.

"Oh, I almost forgot about that," his chief adviser remarked. He continued while smiling, "The great King Abuum of Manaka Kingdom, the wisest king in the heart of Africa."

King Abuum looked at him with a smirk.

Chapter 11

When his friend left, Mbanda sat back to digest the information they had received. He was having mixed feelings; a part of him was happy about the new developments in the Mbantuu Kingdom, another part of him felt a bit jealous that the Mbantuu Kingdom that he had all along shunned, was now in a better place and the person he berated for leaving was actually the one who had helped to solve the kingdom's plight than him. Memories of the last encounter he had with Sango came flashing back to his mind. He felt his words of calling Sango a coward and chicken as applying more to him now, than to Sango. His mood the whole of that day was different even Princess Enieg noticed it and asked if he was alright. He assured her that everything was fine. He wished he could go back to the Mbantuu Kingdom to experience what was happening there, and as well as helping in one way or the other, but the terms on which he left the kingdom were not the best because of that, he was apprehensive about carrying out the idea. He saw an opportunity when Queen Edonge was sending out invitations to the kings to her party. He volunteered to take that of King Mualoko himself to the Mbantuu Kingdom. His request shocked both Queen Edonge and Princess Enieg.

"You want to go to the Mbantuu Kingdom?" Enieg asked.

"Yes, I do," Mbanda replied.

"Why?" she asked.

"Well, it's all but fair that at least I should go there and present it to the king myself since I am married to the princess of this kingdom," Mbanda responded.

"What happened? All these years I have been trying to convince you to go there but you have been adamant about it," Princess Enieg told him.

"Are you sure everything is okay?" she asked concernedly.

Queen Edonge was merely listening to them.

Mbanda replied calmly, "I'm perfectly fine what is the issue, after all, it's my kingdom."

The queen sighed and said, "Well, she is right though. Anyway, since you have decided on your own, you will take the invitation to the King of the Mbantuu Kingdom then," the queen said.

Mbanda nodded his head as he left the room, with both women staring at him as he was leaving. Enieg turned and looked at her mother and said, "Are you sure he is okay, mama?"

Queen Edonge simply shrugged her shoulders and replied, "He seems fine to me, and maybe he has had an epiphany."

Both women continued with what they were doing.

*

Months had gone by since Queen Edonge mentioned to her daughter about her desire to organise a banquet to celebrate the advancement that has been made in her kingdom. She wanted it to be a lavish party, as a result, she had decided that she was not going to rush to organise it but rather to have a well-planned and organised party that met her expectations, and that would forever be remembered in the region. She had sent invitation letters to all the kings in the region both prominent and less prominent kings. When the kings received their invite, they dispatched their guards with presents to offer to the queen ahead of the party, this included herds of cow, sheep, pigs, goats, donkeys and horses. The palace of Shanaba Kingdom was filled with these animals, compelling her to inform her guards to look for somewhere else to keep them. Princess Enieg was thrilled as they were standing and watching how the animals were being led out of the palace premises.

"This is impressive," the queen remarked as she was looking around.

"And the party has not even started," Enieg said.

Mbanda was overseeing the guards as they were moving the animals from the palace, in his company were his children who were excited about seeing the animals.

*

Looking tensely ahead of him, was Mbanda who was in the process of exiting the Shanaba Kingdom enroute to the Mbantuu Kingdom. He had rallied all the Mbantuu warriors who had moved to the Shanaba Kingdom, to accompany him. It's been many years since he last was in the Mbantuu Kingdom. Even though both kingdoms were located in the same region, they were quite far apart. Going to the Mbantuu

Kingdom required several hours of travel often on dangerous roads. As they were travelling, he was a bit anxious, as he did not know what kind of reception he was going to receive. The only thing that comforted him was that he had the other Mbantuu warriors with him. They were all nicely dressed. He had his royal robes on, and a few of the royal guards came along with him. Since he was married to the princess, he automatically was part of the royal family and was treated as such. He could not travel without his royal guards, he did not want to take them along, but the queen insisted that he must have the guards with him. There were altogether twenty-five persons going with him.

Back in the Mbantuu Kingdom, nobody had any clue that he was on his way there. Things were going on smoothly in the kingdom. The residents were going about their normal daily activities. Sango and Mbango had gone to pay Amueh and his family a visit. Sango lived in the interior part of the kingdom while Amueh lived on the outskirts of the kingdom that was closer to the kingdom's entrance. It was a bright day and they had returned from work. They were chatting merrily. In the palace, King Mualoko was with his wife, they were entertaining their daughter who had just returned from a journey with her husband and children. King Mualoko had four children, three girls and a boy. His son was born when he was quite old, so he was much younger than his sisters. He was spoiled for being the king's only son. Since he was the only son of the king, he had to join the Mbantuu warrior group. When Sango returned, he took him under his wings. King Mualoko admired his children and he saw to it that they were a good representation of him and the royal family.

It was getting to the early hours of the evening as Mbanda and his companions were approaching the kingdom's gates. They had travelled the whole day and were tired. Standing at the main gate were four muscular built young men, one of them notified the others when he saw the group of men coming. The four of them became alert as they had been anticipating possible attacks following the discovery of the minerals. One of the guys was told to inform Sango. Following his return from abroad, Sango was asked by the king and his council of elders to take over the group as its commander since most of the prominent men who could lead the group had all travelled out of the kingdom.

He was laughing joyously, when he heard his phone ring. When he saw the number, he sensed something was wrong, he excused himself as he went out to answer the call.

"Hello, yes what is going on?" he said.

"Hello, commander, we have seen a group of men coming towards the kingdom's entrance," the voice informed him.

When he heard this, his heart started to race, he began to think and then asked, "How many are they?"

"They seem to be many, like 15 to 20 or more," the voice told him.

"Okay, good, tell the others to keep calm and to be tactful when the group approach the gates. I will inform the others, I will be coming there soon," Sango said as he ended the call.

He went to join the others, his demeanour showed he had received bad news.

"Is everything okay?" Mbango asked him.

"Yes, but not really, I have just been informed that a group of men are heading towards the kingdom," Sango replied.

Amueh hearing this, stood up and began to ask, "Are they at the kingdom's entrance gates at this moment?"

"Based on what I was told the group is making its way towards the gates, they had not reached the main gate yet," Sango informed them.

"I have to be on my way now to the kingdom's gates," Sango said as he embraced his wife.

"I'm coming with you, we have to defend the kingdom from any foreign attack," Amueh said.

Sango told his wife to stay with Amueh's wife, Eduke, but she wanted to go with him, he objected.

"What about the king?" she asked. "Are you not going to inform him?"

He paused for a moment, and replied, "I have tried to call him, but I could not reach him, so I have asked one of the boys to inform him. I cannot go to the palace now; it is my duty to defend the kingdom. I have the responsibility as the commander of the warrior group to ensure that the kingdom's entrance is protected and defended from any foreign infiltration."

"I will still go there and tell the king," Mbango said.

Sango knew he could not stop her, so he consented to her suggestion as he and Amueh left to go to the kingdom's entrance gate with some reinforcement. He had asked one of the warrior boys to rally all the other boys as they were going to defend the honour of the kingdom.

Making their way towards the kingdom's main entrance was Sango, he knew the warrior boys had seen them. When they got closer to the gates, he asked his guards to stop as he descended with his boys. When he got down, he began looking around observing the environment. One of the

Shanaba guards asked if he needed protection, to which he declined. He proceeded to walk majestically towards the guards who were standing with their weapons. As he was getting closer, he greeted them in the Mbantuu language.

"Chanmukan," he said.

When the guards heard this, they turned and looked at each other. They did not reply.

Mbanda greeted them again. One of the warriors asked authoritatively.

"Who are you and what do you want?"

"Calm down my brothers, I am a Mbantuu resident. I am a son of Mbantuu Kingdom," Mbanda replied.

The other Mbantuu warriors came behind him when he said that. He looked at them and turned to the warriors guarding the entrance gates and said, "We are all children of Mbantuu Kingdom."

His entourage yelled, "Chan'mukan."

The guards were still feeling sceptical, they knew they looked like people from their kingdom, but they were apprehensive. They were contemplating whether to let them in. Seeing that they were hesitant, Mbanda opened his shirt and showed his lion tattoo, and the others did the same.

"Ah warriors, they are our fellow warriors!" the young men exclaimed.

They let their guard down and went to shake hands with Mbanda and the others. They were in the process of exchanging pleasantries when Sango arrived with Amueh and a group of armed warriors. He asked one of the guards to open the gates as he was informed that the men in question were Mbantuu natives. They stood waiting inside as they watched Mbanda, and his men make their way into the kingdom. When they got in and saw Sango and the others, Mbanda asked his men to stop, as he walked towards Sango and Amueh. He adjusted his clothes which were colourful royal robes, as he walked majestically. He wanted to exude an air of royalty as his guards were walking behind him. Sango turned and looked at Amueh. Amueh simply nodded his head.

"Chan'mukan," Mbanda said as he got closer to them.

Sango could barely recognise him; he looked a bit different. He looked older and much bigger than the last time he saw him.

"Chan'mukan," both Sango and Amueh replied.

"I know you might be wondering, who is this person greeting you?"

"Not at all, I know who you are," Sango said emphatically.

"Do you? Well, that is nice," Mbanda replied.

"So, what brought you here Mbanda?" Sango asked him.

"What kind of question is that, is this not my kingdom? I am a Mbantuu resident," Mbanda replied.

"So, the prodigal son has returned," Sango said with sarcasm.

When he heard this, Mbanda chuckled and said, "The same can be said about you."

"Well, I have heard about all your illicit abhorrent activities that had contributed to tarnishing the reputation and image of our beloved kingdom, worst of all your bastardisation of the warrior group," Sango said.

"Is that all they told you?" Mbanda asked nonchalantly.

"I'm sure there are many more, but that is the least of my interest," Sango said. "So, you did not stay back and help the kingdom after all?"

"I had more important things to attend to," Mbanda replied.

"I bet you did, who was the coward and chicken then?" Sango asked while looking at him in the face.

Mbanda could not say anything, his pride would not let him admit that he was wrong. He knew what Sango was saying was right. On the way, he was planning on apologising to Sango but now that he was facing him, he was finding it difficult to voice it out.

"See, I left this kingdom many years ago, I cannot blame you for leaving as well since you had your dreams and plan. Good and nice, but one thing that I have longed to tell you is that neither am I a coward nor am I a chicken. So, you should get that into your head," Sango said between clenched teeth.

"Okay, good and fine, you are not a coward, you are not a chicken," Mbanda said stuttering. He continued, "I'm not the old Mbanda anymore, I have changed. I must admit I was wrong about you. We had our differences in the past but now I'm not like that anymore."

While staring at him, Sango began to walk around him, he was finding it hard to believe what he was saying, he stopped and said, "Good and fine, if you say so, but we will have to see that. You know that I don't rely on people's words but their actions."

"See, I have changed. I came here to renew my relationship with my kinsmen and to see the king," Mbanda said.

"Oh, you did not come because you heard of the changes taking place in Mbantuu?" Sango asked.

"To be honest, partly," Mbanda said slowly.

Sango looked at him and said loudly, "Wow, you have really changed. So, you are no longer led by your muscles and greed."

"Can I go and see the king now?" Mbanda asked impatiently.

Sango looked at him and his boys, he paused for a while and replied, "Well, if your intentions are good, you can go and see the king, but he is the one to permit your return to this kingdom."

Sango indicated to the warrior boys to lead them to the palace.

As they were leaving, Sango turned and said, "Hey Mbanda, one more thing, don't try to play any funny games in this kingdom or have any hidden ulterior motives because I will personally kill you."

"Is that a threat?" Mbanda asked.

"No, it is not. It is a warning, I don't make threats," Sango said.

King Mualoko was in a good mood as he was in the company of his family, when Mbango came to the palace to inform him about the group of unknown men heading to the kingdom. She was in a frantic state when she got to the palace. The king was surprised to see her and was wondering if something had happened to Sango. When she informed him about the men, the king immediately asked his guards to inform members of his council of advisers and to rally all the warrior boys to the king's palace. However, he was informed by his guards that Sango had already rallied the warrior group. His wife and children were asked to hide in a secret room that was in the palace.

Mbanda and his group were walking slowly as people were coming out of their houses to see who they were. It had been a long time since strangers visited the kingdom. They were wondering who they were, in order to relieve their fears, some of the men had to speak to the people in their Mbantuu language. They also met some armed Mbantuu warriors on their way, some of the men accompanying Mbanda stopped to have a chat with them. It turned out that they actually knew some of them. They happily embraced each other, some were really thrilled that they wanted to continue chatting, but Mbanda insisted that all of them have to go to the king's palace together. Mbanda was looking around as he saw the different changes that had taken place in the kingdom. The big lion sculpture that was placed in the centre of the market square was made of gold and was shining brightly under the sun. The group of men stopped to have a look at it. It was gigantic. Mbanda was impressed by what he was seeing. When they finally arrived at the king's palace, they were stopped by the palace guards. Mbanda got down and began talking to them in the Mbantuu language, in the process of talking, he introduced himself and informed them that he desires to see the king. When King Mualoko was told about the presence of Mbanda, he was wondering what had brought him back, but he was a bit relieved because they had anticipated that it would be an invasion attempt by foreigners.

When he was in the king's presence, Mbanda was much humbler than the king and his advisers remembered him to be.

"Mbanda, you came out of the blue and decided to come back to Mbantuu? Have you stopped running or is it because the kingdom is no longer a derelict and hopeless kingdom?" King Mualoko asked.

"My king, I must admit I made a mistake when I was young, I had not been the most respectful and sensible warrior, but I have changed," Mbanda said.

"Hmm, we heard you got married to the princess of Shanaba Kingdom, as I can see from your clothes." One of the men remarked.

"Yes, I did, that is part of the reason I'm here today," Mbanda informed him.

The chief adviser asked, "What could that mean?"

"The Queen of Shanaba has sent a letter of invitation to the King of Mbantuu Kingdom," Mbanda said.

"For what?" King Mualoko asked.

"Well, she is planning to organise a party to celebrate the progress of her kingdom, and she would love to have all the kings in the region at the party," Mbanda said as he went towards the king to hand him the invitation letter.

King Mualoko took it from him and began to read it.

After reading it he bends forward and said, "I hope Mbanda this is not a setup because I know news about the new fortune that has been discovered in our kingdom must have spread far and wide."

"It is not a setup, my king," Mbanda assured him.

"It better not be, because I will not be held responsible for what will happen to you and the Queen of Shanaba if it turns out to be." The king said in a threatening tone.

"You can rest assured about that," Mbanda said.

"Well, if you say so, you have in the past proved to be untrustworthy, but since you say you have changed, we will give you the benefit of a doubt," King Mualoko said.

"So, are you called a prince now?" one of the advisers asked.

"Yes, I am," Mbanda replied.

"My king, will you grant us the permission to come back to the Mbantuu Kingdom?" Mbanda asked.

King Mualoko sat quietly as he was thinking about what he said.

"Are you people no longer enjoying your stay in Shanaba Kingdom? Is it no longer a Paradise? Moreover, there is not enough space for you, the kingdom has expanded and there are many more people now," the chief adviser, who was irritated, said.

"We did not exile you, you people decided to exile yourselves. You people are welcome back if you want to," King Mualoko told him.

Mbanda hearing this began to smile. "Thank you, my king."

"But on the condition that you undergo a readmission test that would require you to prove your trustworthiness and commitment to this kingdom. We don't want any problems. Any confrontation between you and your group will not be tolerated in any shape or form. The first time you left easily but this time around you won't be able to do so."

Chapter 12

When King Abuum received his invitation, he was quite apprehensive because he was not certain if it was authentic or a set-up. He was not certain Queen Edonge was particularly interested in having a friendly relationship between her kingdom and his, based on her reaction when he paid her a visit. He knew he could not blame her, he even considered her to be much more civil than he anticipated, when considering the tension and conflict that had characterised the relationship between both kingdoms. He was not too sure of what to make about the invitation. *'Could it be a set-up?'* he said to himself.

Days later, when he had a meeting with his advisers, he brought up the topic about the invitation he received from the Queen of Shanaba Kingdom. When the men heard this, almost all the men were sceptical about it. Some of them raised the point that it was probably a plot aimed at trapping the king. They believed it was a strategy by the queen to avenge the death of her husband. While the men were talking, King Abuum sat quietly as he was looking at them. He noticed that two of the men were not engaged in the conversation with the other men.

"My chief adviser has not made known his opinion on the matter at hand," King Abuum said.

Where he was sitting the chief adviser replied, "I think it is a good idea, I don't believe there is any malicious intention behind the invitation."

"How are you sure?" one of the men asked him.

"It could be a ploy by the queen. Let's not forget what happened between our kingdom and her kingdom. Why would she invite a king from a kingdom that killed her husband and destroyed her kingdom? Think about it," one of the men remarked.

"Well, you people have a point, but I think the Queen of is a wise woman, killing the King of Manaka Kingdom would be the last thing she may have on her mind, what would it do to her? It won't help her much. I sincerely reckon she is more interested in building her kingdom as opposed to waging war with other kingdoms."

"That is just wishful thinking, don't forget that her daughter is married to one brute from the Mbantuu Kingdom, he might have corrupted her mind in orchestrating this whole party thing," one of the men said.

King Abuum after hearing their take on the issue informed them.

"I will be attending the party, we are all assuming, and I do side with what Molua said. I will go to the party and see what she has in store for me."

*

Back in the Mbantuu Kingdom, King Mualoko was discussing with his wife Queen Anieh about what they should take along as a present to give to Queen Edonge.

"Maybe you can take some of the *Nnam* and offer it to her. Since they are stones that are rare and are not found in the other kingdoms," his wife suggested.

He was quiet for some minutes and then said, "It is a good idea; however, I have to discuss it with my advisers." Days later, following his consultation with his council of advisers, it was concluded that he should take some pieces of the precious stones with him to the Queen of Shanaba as a present from the people of the Mbantuu Kingdom.

Things were relatively calm in the heart of Africa. The region was experiencing peace and tranquillity, which had never been the case in the past. The region had always been characterised by the occurrence of frequent conflicts and wars between the different kingdoms that make up the region. This level of tranquillity that was prevailing in the region could be considered to be an anomaly, if one was making judgments based on how things used to be in the region in the past. Although the different kingdoms were secretly plotting against each other, there was not any overt antagonisation between the kingdoms. King Abuum was busy planning his grandiose idea of expanding the Manaka Kingdom into an empire; King Mualoko was deeply involved in there construction of the fallen Mbantuu Kingdom; Queen Edonge in addition to planning to organise a huge luxurious party that had never been organised in the region, was as well overseeing the transformation of the Shanaba Kingdom following the defeat it suffered at the hands of the Manaka Kingdom; King Duu of the Utanne Kingdom on his part was simply contented with the progress of his kingdom as well as having finally had the opportunity of establishing a relationship with Shanaba and Manaka kingdoms. Everything was, to say the least, positive for the most part in the region. However, in a far distant land beyond the borders of Africa, the future of the region was being discussed.

*

Much to the unawareness of the kings in the heart of Africa, a group of men were holding a discussion about the fortune of the region.

"These kingdoms possess great wealth which we need. We have to go there and exploit these resources," one man said.

"Yes, we have to, but those kingdoms are strong and powerful, it will not be an easy task to defeat them," one of the men remarked.

"We have powerful weapons, which we can use," one of the men said.

Amongst the group of men discussing in the meeting were the four men who had gone to the Manaka Kingdom. The older man began to speak.

"We have tried to buy the resources, but the King of Manaka Kingdom objected to it. In the past, we have been able to manipulate the kings and they gave us these resources without any major hesitation but now, I think that will not be possible."

"You are right, my friend," another man said.

"Since they don't want to sell nor need any assistance, we have no other option but to use forceful measures."

One of the men who went to the Manaka Kingdom asked, "But how are we going to do this? Should we start by invading the kingdoms separately?"

"No, that won't be a good idea, because the news will spread, and the other kingdoms will become aware of our presence and prepare for us. We have to take them by surprise."

The old man added, "The first thing we need to do is eliminate the kings because they possess a lot of power in the kingdoms, their authority is supreme and greatly respected. If they are eliminated, this will plunge the kingdoms into a state of chaos."

The men sat quietly for some minutes then one said, "A little bird whispered to me a while ago that the Queen of Shanaba Kingdom is planning to organise a huge party that all the kings in the region will attend, all the top kings in the region."

This information was joyously received by the other men in the meeting.

"Brilliant, good information, that is our great opportunity to strike, Ah! There is our unique chance to eliminate them," one of the men yelled.

All the men were elated that they knew that their plan was going to be propitious. Knowing that the party will be filled with the dead bodies of the kings of the heart of Africa, felt sweet to them. In essence, they believe this will mark the end of the reign of these kingdoms in the region and subsequently pave the way for them to come in and grab the resources they had longed to possess, without any objection whatsoever.

*

Days have gone by, and the day that Queen Edonge had planned to organise her party was fast approaching. All the kings were kind of looking forward to it. There had not previously been any meeting in the history of the region where all the kings were in the same venue together. Although the kings at the back of their mind, had some apprehension to attend the party, they had decided individually to proceed with caution. All of them were thinking of not going to the party without their top warrior boys as a backup in case of any unexpected circumstance arising.

After his visit to the Mbantuu Kingdom, Mbanda went back to the Shanaba Kingdom feeling relieved that the visit turned out better than he anticipated. It felt like a huge weight had been lifted off his shoulders. His wife and the queen were pleased to hear about it. Back in the Mbantuu Kingdom, King Mualoko was discussing with Sango about the party at the Shanaba Kingdom, he informed him that he would like him to accompany him there.

"I think I need some warrior boys to come along as well to the party for safety purposes. I don't really trust if the party is really genuine or if it is a decoy for something else," King Mualoko said.

Sango after hearing his concern replied, "I reckon it is a good idea even though I feel it is just a party. But one can't be too sure how the other kings are thinking. It is always better to be safe than sorry."

"That's right, if King Abuum of Manaka Kingdom will be there, you know I can't really vouch on how he will react. One can't go to the market empty-handed and expect to return with a full basket."

"Oh, my king, I have heard your concerns, I will inform some of the top warrior boys about this. Mbanda told me he would appreciate it if I came to the party with my wife, as well as Amueh.”

King Mualoko seemed stunned by what he said.

“Really? Did he actually ask you to come?” King Mualoko asked.

Sango replied, “Yes, he did. His request surprised me.”

“Hmm, it seems he has changed indeed, who would have known. Marriage has done wonders on him,” King Mualoko said.

Sango began to laugh, he then said, “My king, you know what they say, a woman can change the most dangerous brute to a charming prince.”

Both men continued to laugh.

Chapter 13

Queen Edonge was in the company of some of her dearest friends, as they were talking about the party. From afar, one could hear their laughter. She was looking forward to seeing the dress that had been specially designed for her to wear at the party. One of her maids came with a package that contained the gown. The queen was quite enchanted when her maid brought the package. When the women saw the package, one of them hurriedly took it from the maid and began opening it. It was along gown that was embroidered in gold and red.

She had everything planned for the party, everything was moving smoothly as she expected. She had earlier during the day gone to the venue where the party was to be held. The whole kingdom was in a festive mood, everybody was looking forward to it. Although all the residents of the kingdom were not to attend the main party, small parties were to be organised in different parts of the kingdom. This was intended to ensure that people who were not going to attend the main party attended by the queen and kings, could also celebrate. The central part of the main city in the kingdom was beautifully decorated with prominent crafts that are unique to the kingdom.

While the queen was admiring her dress with her friends, she heard a knock on the door, a maid came into the room in which they were sitting with a package in her hands. The women turned and looked, it was a huge package, it was nicely parcelled, and they were looking curiously at it. Queen Edoneg asked, "Binze, what is that?"

"Your majesty, it is a present brought by one guard from the Utanne Kingdom."

The queen a bit bemused, took the parcel from her and was about to open it, when the maid said, "There is also a present sent by King Abuum of Manaka Kingdom."

Queen Edonge was staggered. "Hmm, Oh really? He sent a present?"

The other women began laughing. "Why is he sending you presents?" one of her friends asked.

"Hmm, I wonder why, that man is a character," the queen replied.

She began opening the parcel. In it was a huge necklace, and earnings. She took the pieces of jewellery from the package and began to look at them, her friends were marvelled at the sight of it.

"They look gorgeous and expensive," they said.

The queen herself was impressed, "I have not seen such beautiful jewellery."

"Can you try it on?" one of the women asked.

"Why not?" she replied.

They helped to wear it on her neck.

"Oh, Queen Edonge you look radiant!"

A mirror was brought to her, so that she could see how it looked on her.

"Well, I must confess, the man has a good taste," Dialle said.

"Yes, he sure does," Queen Edonge concurred.

"Someone really likes you," Mpunde remarked.

"He sure does," Queen Edonge said.

All the women burst out laughing.

*

In the different kingdoms, the kings were preparing for their departure for the Shanaba Kingdom. Sango along with his wife and King Mualoko and his wife, as well as Amueh and his wife were as well prepared. They were going along with the king's chief adviser and a couple of the warrior boys who were selected by Sango. Mbango had asked one of the maids to watch over Seme and Mbone while they were away. She was packing the dress she planned to wear at the party. She had earlier worn it to show Sango.

"Wow, you look beautiful!" Sango told her.

"Do you like it?" Mbango asked.

"The dress looks lovely," Sango told her.

She was happy that he liked it.

"Let's hurry, soon we will be leaving," she informed Sango.

The different guests from the different kingdoms had arrived at the Shanaba Kingdom a day before the party was to take place. Queen Edonge had named it "*Nlatan*" which meant union party. The accommodation was made available for all the invited guests. Since the distance between the kingdoms was far apart, the guests had to arrive a day before. Princess Enieg and Mbanda were at the head of the organising committee. Enieg was ensuring that everything was properly planned and the venue beautifully decorated.

Sango and Mbango, and the king and his wife shared the same hotel along with the chief adviser, and Amueh and Eduke. The warrior boys were shown somewhere else to stay. Mbango was feeling a bit sad that she had left the children but at the same time, she was anxious about attending the party, because she had never been to the Shanaba Kingdom. She had heard great tales about the women of the kingdom. She was curious to see the queen and her daughter.

"There is a lot being said about the Queen of the Shanaba Kingdom and her daughter. It seems like she has the spirit of the goddess of the heart of Africa," Mbango said.

Sango who was busy packing his things was barely paying attention to what she was saying, simply responded, "Hmm, so I heard."

"Have you met her before?" she asked.

"Have I met her? Hmm, I think once but it was a long time ago," Sango responded reluctantly.

"Hmm, is she really that gorgeous like everyone is saying?" she asked.

"It has been a long time, I can't remember well—" Sango said and then he added "—yes, she is."

Mbango was about to say something else when they heard a knock on the door. It was King Mualoko's guard who had come to inform them that the king was waiting for them. Sango was relieved. What he had failed to mention to Mbango was that he had met Queen Edonge more than once. That was a long time ago when he was younger. He had travelled with the king to the Shanaba Kingdom that was when he came across Queen Edonge, but she was not the queen then. She was young and not married then, she had liked him even though she was older than him, but Sango was not too keen on having a relationship with her. They had planned that Sango would come by to the Shanaba Kingdom later, but Sango never showed up and this angered her.

*

The sun was shining brightly outside, Princess Enieg and Mbanda had already dressed up. Mbanda was looking at Enieg as she was twirling in her gown, feeling very happy with her dress.

"You look exquisite," Mbanda said to her.

She was thrilled when she heard this.

"I am a lucky man," Mbanda said. "Who would have known that I will be married to a princess like you? I will kill any man who tries to take you away from me."

"Hush dear, you don't have to be dramatic," Enieg told him. "Come let's go, my mother must be waiting, and you know she does not like to wait for anybody."

Although Enieg was younger than him, she was a very strong-willed, determined and head strong person.

The queen came down the palace hall where Enieg and Mbanda were waiting for her.

"Wow, Mother, you look amazing," Enieg said as her mother was walking towards her.

"My queen, you look stunning," Eduke her friend, said.

"Those kings would be panting like dogs," Mbanda said.

"Oh Mbanda, my beloved son in law, thanks for the compliment," Queen Edonge said while smiling.

They all made their way out of the palace.

All the kings were in the venue where the party was held, except King Abuum. Everybody looked elegant and sophisticated. Music was being played in the background by the royal orchestral, as some men and women were dancing to entertain the guests. Drinks were being served to the guests. Sango, Mbango, Amueh and his wife, Molua along with King Mualoko and Queen Anieh had made their way into the party venue. Mbango looked beautiful in her dress, she was enjoying the decorations and arrangements made in the venue. They went and began to mingle with the other guests. King Mualoko was in the company of King Duu talking when King Abuum made his entrance. In his usual style, he liked to make a grand entrance. When he saw the other kings, he began to walk confidently towards them, pulling along his huge embroidered flowing robe.

"Gentlemen. It is good to see you, people," he said.

"Welcome! King Abuum, the king of the rising kingdom," King Duu said teasingly.

"Come on my friend, the giant kingdom in the heart of Africa, no offence, King Mualoko," King Abuum said while laughing.

"None taken," King Mualoko replied smiling.

"Gentlemen, in fact, it is the first time we are all in the same place at the same time," King Abuum remarked.

"Yes indeed, this has never happened before," King Mualoko said.

"Hats off to the Queen of Shanaba Kingdom. She did something that we the men and the kings have not been able to do," King Duu said.

"That is why they said she is the goddess of the heart of Africa, what a woman!" King Abuum said.

As the men were talking, they were joined by other kings from smaller kingdoms. Everybody was waiting anxiously for the arrival of Queen Edonge.

Chapter 14

Everybody was feeling merry; the different kings were looking around as they were in awe of what they were seeing.

"I must confess the queen has done a marvellous job. When I came here, I could not believe my eyes at the development that has taken place," King Abuum said.

"She is a strong woman," King Mualoko said.

"I now understand why she is referred to as the goddess of the heart of Africa," King Duu remarked.

King Abuum then said, "King Mualoko I heard about the great fortune that has happened in your kingdom."

"It is the work of the gods," King Mualoko replied.

"It is something nice," King Duu told him.

"We have been through a lot," King Mualoko said to them.

As they were talking, Queen Edonge and Princess Enieg were making their entrance to the venue. The attention of all the guests shifted towards them, everybody turned and was looking at them. Sango and Mbango as well turned and began to look at them.

"Wow, they are beautiful," Mbango said.

"Yes, they are," concurred Eduke.

Sango simply nodded his head, he was staring at them as they were walking towards their direction, he was trying to hide his face so that the queen should not see him, but little did he know that she had already spotted him from afar. Mbanda, seeing them, stopped as he proceeded to greet them.

"Chan'mukan," he said as he extended his hand to greet them.

"It is such an honour to meet the famous Queen of Shanaba Kingdom," Mbango said with enthusiasm.

"Likewise, and you are?" Queen Edonge asked.

"Mbango," she replied.

Sango was looking at Mbango affectionately while she was talking with the queen. Queen Edonge while squinting said, "You look kind of familiar. I'm wondering if we have met before?"

Sango was about to reply when Mbanda who was busy talking to some guests turned towards them and said, "Sango this is my wife, Princess Enieg."

While they were talking, King Abuum came walking towards them and the queen's attention shifted to him. They began to talk as they were walking towards their seats that were reserved for them. While she was walking away, the queen turned and looked at Sango, she then asked Mbanda, "What is his name?"

"Who?" Mbanda asked.

"The guy from the Mbantuu Kingdom," she said.

"Sango, he was or is the commander of the Mbantuu warrior group," Mbanda replied.

The queen then muttered softly, "Ah, I knew it!"

"What did you say, my queen?" Mbanda asked.

"No, nothing, never mind," she replied as they continued to walk to their seats.

Following the arrival of the queen and her entourage, the party officially started. All the guests took their seats. They were chatting, laughing and drinking. While everybody was in a festive mode, they were oblivious of the potential attack that was to take place. Making their way to the kingdom, were a group of armed men, amongst them were the four men who had visited King Abuum sometime ago. The group was led by the old man.

They were planning to reach the kingdom before sunset because they wanted to be there before the different kings departed the party venue.

Back at the party, King Duu had asked Queen Edonge for a dance. She was enjoying herself, but she was secretly looking in Sango's direction.

"Did you like the present?" King Duu asked.

Lost in her thoughts the queen responded, "Ah, yes, I did. Thanks for it, sorry I did not thank you earlier, pardon my manners."

"It is okay my queen, I have plenty more for you," King Duu replied.

As they were busy talking, King Abuum came by and interrupted them, to the dismay of King Duu.

"If you do not mind, I would like to have a dance with the queen," King Abuum said.

"Sure, of course," King Duu said grumpily.

The queen was merely looking at them, smiling. She secretly loved the attention the men were giving her.

King Duu left and as he went to ask for Mbango's hand for a dance. She was talking with Sango and did not see him approach them. She was reluctant, she turned and looked at Sango, he nodded his head indicating it was okay. Seeing that he was alone, Queen Edonge while dancing with King Abuum, came up with an excuse that she wanted to go to the restroom to refresh herself. She walked to the restroom on her way back; she began to make her way towards Sango. Sango, seeing her coming, stood still, he did not know what to do, and he looked around him to make sure Mbango was not watching. Amueh was dancing with Eduke.

"Sango, right?" she asked.

Sango nodded his head.

"I knew I had seen you before," she said.

"Yes, good to see you again," Sango responded.

"Likewise," Queen Edonge said.

"I know it is kind of uncomfortable. I did not know you were the queen," Sango said.

"Ah, no big deal. Yes, it's been a long time, so many years. Do you want to dance?" she asked.

Sango replied reluctantly, "Well, I don't think it will be a good idea or appropriate, you are the queen."

"And so? You are married," she said. "Your wife is beautiful, she looks stunning," she told him.

"Thanks," Sango responded.

"Come on, it is just a dance, I am not going to snatch you away from your wife, it is a party, I have forgotten about you not coming back like you had promised," she said to him.

"I'm sorry about that," Sango said.

"It's okay it was not meant to be," the queen told him. "Come let's dance."

Sango finally gave in to her request and they walked to the dance floor.

"I don't want the kings to be jealous," Sango said.

"Don't worry yourself about that. If they are, that will be great," she said. "You look good."

"Thanks, you too," Sango responded.

Sango turned and looked at Mbango, she was in a good mood.

It looked like she was enjoying herself. She looked towards his direction and waved at him, and he waved back.

As he was turning his head to face the queen, a loud sound could be heard coming from outside, the ground began to tremble. The hall turned into a chaotic state as the frantic voices of the guests could be heard. The whole place was in a frenzy as everybody was in a frightened state, as screams of women could be heard from afar. Sango turned and looked towards Mbango, he tried to shield the queen as her guards rushed towards her and took her away. Sango immediately rushed towards Mbango. He took her to a corner of the room to ensure that she was safe. He was followed by Amueh and his wife. The guards of the different kings were leading them to a place of safety. Sango spotted some of the warrior boys who had entered the building, he instructed them to protect King Mualoko and his wife. Mbanda came towards Sango, and they began to talk. He informed them that they need to move the kings and the queen and the other top royal guests to one of the secret rooms that were in the building. He ordered the guards to proceed to do this.

"I think we are under attack," Mbanda said in a loud voice.

As they were talking Amueh and some of the warrior boys came into the hall to inform them what was actually happening. They informed them that some groups of men were responsible for the attack. The men decided to talk with the leaders of the warrior groups of the different kingdoms and to come up with a strategy to fight back, protect and defend the kingdom. The commander leading the Manaka warrior group, named Ngede and Zuum came by and met them, they all came up with a plan on how to counter the attack. Mbanda ringed for backup warriors to come to the venue. The sounds of guns were heard coming from different directions. The guests were screaming in fright. Sango and others took their weapons as they headed to fight the invaders.

After several minutes of fighting between the two camps, the sounds of gunshots began to die down. Sango and the others had fought fiercely against the intruders. Some of the men were retreating, leaving behind their weapons. As the men were trying to escape, they were intercepted by some Shanaba guards who killed most of the men. They succeeded in capturing four of the men, and they led them into the venue which was in shambles, as they met Sango and the others. Sango, Amueh, Mbanda and Zuum came out when they saw the guards coming with the men. They were looking around at the destruction that had been caused, some of the guests had been killed during the crossfire. They were trying to help some of the guests that were injured. The female guards of the Shanaba Kingdom were told by Mbanda to take care of them. The men captured were severely wounded and they were being pulled along by the guards and brought in front of Sango and the others. They were moaning in pain, because of the wounds they had sustained. One of the men began to plead to them to spare their lives.

"Spare your lives after you people have caused the death of innocent people?" Sango yelled at them as he took his gun and shot him.

The two men began to tremble in fear.

"Please don't kill us," the men pleaded.

"If we let you go you should never come back to this region, ever again," Mbanda said angrily.

Then he grabbed one of the men and looked at him in the face and said, "Why did you people come here?"

The man began to stutter. "We wanted to gain control of the resources in the heart of Africa. That is why we decided to come to the Shanaba Kingdom to kill the kings."

"Really? Did you people discover any minerals here?" Sango asked them.

"No, no we didn't," they answered.

Then Ngede noticed one of the men.

"I think I have seen you before, hmm, you were amongst the men that came to the Manaka Kingdom to buy some minerals."

The man nodded his head in confirmation.

Sango bent down and looked at them and said, "We are going to spare your lives today on account that you people should go back and tell your people to never, I mean ever try such an atrocious act again in the entire region."

He chuckled. "The next time—" he paused and looked at the other men behind him and continued "—the next time we see your faces around this region, you won't be so lucky."

"Thank you," the men trembling said.

"Now be gone," Sango yelled at them.

The men struggled to get up as they proceeded to walk away.

"We should have killed them," Amueh said.

"Let them go, I don't think they will make it far. They are severely wounded. They will take the message back to their people, wherever they are from."

"With the gangs on the roads, I doubt they will make it to their place of origin," Mbanda remarked.

With the men out of sight, Sango and the others went into the building where all the guests and kings were, the sounds of guns could no longer be heard. All the kings and Queen Edonge were brought out from where they were hiding by their guards. The surviving guests were all in raptures that the men had been defeated, even though they were still terrified by what had happened. Queen Edonge was sad that such an attack had taken place at her party and in her kingdom. She was a bit livid that her party had ended in such a horrific way, however, she was relieved that they were still alive. Princess Enieg, Mbango and Eduke went to embrace their husbands. The kings commented on Sango and the others for crushing the attack.

"You see what collaboration can do," King Duu remarked.

"Yes, you are totally right, the joint forces of all our kingdoms were able to halt and defeat the foreigners," King Abuum mentioned. "That is something we should do often. It is a lesson we should learn from this ordeal."

"That is exactly what we require in this region. We have much to gain if we work together as opposed to fighting and engaging in senseless conflicts," King Mualoko said.

Queen Edonge sorrowfully said, "Sorry gentlemen that the party did not have a great ending, like I anticipated, but I hope we all can come together some other time in the future. And hopefully, there won't be any unexpected attacks."

"That is rightly said, Queen Edonge, although some lives were lost, but it was a pleasure being here today," King Abuum assured her.

Months later after the party organised by Queen Edonge, there was blissfulness in the region. Following the defeat of the foreigners, the different kings had set up strategies in their respective kingdoms with the intention to preclude any unexpected attack from foreigners. Safeguarding the territorial borders of the kingdoms had been a top priority for the kings, as they did not want what happened in Shanaba Kingdom to repeat itself. They all jointly came to a consensus that in case of such an attack or threat against any of the kingdoms, they would provide backup support. This, they deem will ensure better security in the region not only for the individual kingdoms but for the entire heart of the African region. This sort of agreement had never been reached previously in the region. Steps were taken towards ensuring that the new partnership between the different regions was in place.

To commemorate the day that tides turned in favour of things in the Mbantuu Kingdom, King Mualoko and his advisers decided to organise a ceremony, where all the different kings and Queen Edonge of Shanaba Kingdom were invited to attend. The event was also seen as a medium to mark the new phase in the relationship between the different kingdoms in the heart of Africa. Everyone in the Mbantuu Kingdom was looking forward to it. Mbone and Seme were excited when Sango had informed them about it. Sango's relationship with Mbanda had become better. They had been on great terms, much better than they have ever been. Everything in the Mbantuu Kingdom was in a great state than it had ever been. The conditions were marvellous. When he travelled across the kingdom, he was pleasantly impressed by what had taken place, he himself could not believe his eyes of the achievements that had been made. King Mualoko could not wait to show the other kings the transformation that his kingdom had undergone.

On the day of the event, the Mbantuu Kingdom was in a festive state, as the different kings were received and taken to the ceremonial ground. Queen Edonge arrived with Mbanda and Princess Enieg and their children. It was the first time they were visiting the Mbantuu Kingdom, they were quite impressed. The children were in raptures as they were for the first time, in the kingdom their father hailed from. At the ceremonial ground, they met Sango's children and they instantly became friends. Sango, Mbanda, Amueh, Ngede as well as Zuum were sitting in the same place, while Mbango, Amueh's wife and Princess Enieg were busy chatting with each other. The kings: King Mualoko, King Abuum, King Duu and Queen Edonge and some other kings from the smaller kingdoms, were also busy discussing amongst themselves. They were all laughing.

"Who would have imagined that all the kingdoms in the heart of Africa would get along?" Sango remarked as he was hearing the laughter of the kings.

"Never in my wildest dream would I have thought this would ever happen," Mbanda said.

"It is funny how things have turned out," Amueh said.

"Yes indeed," Zuum said. "I wouldn't have thought I would be friends with you guys, especially with you Mbanda."

Mbanda and the others smiled.

"Well, let's hope things stay this way forever," Sango said.

"And that no foreigner should attempt to take what is rightfully ours."

"This is what the heart of Africa should be all about, love, peace and partnership," Sango said.

The kings overheard what he said, and they turned towards their direction, "Let's toast to what Sango said," King Mualoko said.

"To a new phase in the history of the heart of Africa," King Mualoko said.

"Let peace, unity and solidarity reign between our kingdoms and the other kingdoms in the region," King Abuum said. "Does the queen have anything to add?"

"Sure, of course," she said while smiling. "Gentlemen, oh I forgot ladies first," as she turned and looked at the other women around, who were laughing.

"Together let's make the heart of Africa, the best place to be, no more conflicts and wars in the heart of Africa," she said in her usual elegant manner.

Everybody raised their glasses in the air, with a smile on their faces.

www.ingramcontent.com/pod-product-compliance
Lightning Source LLC
Chambersburg PA
CBHW061528050726

47593CB00002B/710